The Spy Who Kissed Me

The Spy Who Kissed Me

Pauline Baird Jones

Five Star
Unity, Maine

This novel is a work of fiction. Names, characters, places, and incidents are either the product of the author's imagination, or, if real, used fictitiously.

Five Star First Edition Romance, Second Printing.
Published in conjunction with Pauline Baird Jones

April 2000
Five Star Standard Print First Edition Romance Series.

The text of this edition is unabridged.

Set in 11 pt. Plantin by Rick Gundberg.

Printed in the United States on permanent paper.

Library of Congress Cataloging-in-Publication Data

Jones, Pauline Baird.
The spy who kissed me / Pauline Baird Jones. — Five Star 1st. ed. romance, stand. print hardcover ed.
p. cm. — (Five Star standard print first edition romance series)
ISBN 0-7862-2413-4 (hc : alk. paper)
I. Title. II. Series.
PS3560.O52415 S69 2000
813′.54—dc21 99-088109

This book is dedicated to my husband, Greg, who
believed in me even when I didn't believe in myself.
Thanks, honey.

Chapter One

I'd never have gotten mixed up in the first murder if Mrs. MacPhearson hadn't caught the flu, but I can't blame her for a capricious fate rolling the "who's turn is it to be smitten?" dice and my name—Isabel Stanley—coming up.

Isabel. Picture someone petite, fragile and blonde, done in soft pastels, lusciously formed—and you'll know how I *don't* look. Most people find it less stressful to call me Stan when faced with a reality that is tall, lots of leg, and colored in brown and pasty white . . . with crayons.

Don't get me wrong. Being darn near invisible isn't the worst thing that can happen to you. Ask my twin sister Rosemary about her ex. Just be sure to do it from a safe distance. Calling her spitting mad isn't an exercise in the theoretical.

I used to be a safe distance from her and my mother until six months ago when my instinct for survival got swamped by guilt because my sister's divorce happened to coincide with our dad's abrupt exit from this life. Since my livelihood is done with computer and sketch pad for the benefit of slightly dysfunctional children, I was able to make the move from New Orleans to Arlington, Virginia almost painlessly.

Painless isn't possible with my mother in the mix. She's a fundamentalist Baptist and thinks that authoring a roach named Cochran, no matter how spunky and cute, is just tacky. That it pays very well only adds insult to her imagined injury.

With that attitude, there's no way I'm telling her about my secret yearning to add romance writing to my roach credits. It won't be an issue for some time. Romance novels are hard to write and being raised by said Fundamental Baptist isn't the best preparation for writing love scenes.

Not too surprisingly, our fractured little family was rubbing along about as smoothly as chalk on a blackboard when Mrs. MacPhearson got the flu, sending my life screeching off into a dangerous—and embarrassing—new direction.

I had no premonition of impending danger when I said I'd fill in for Mrs. M during the youth choir practice. I like playing the organ and they have hot chocolate afterwards. Gourmet hot chocolate. They have to. It's January in our tiny suburb of DC and our church is old and cold. If circulation isn't restored quickly, frostbite is inevitable.

Since I have an aversion to freezing to death and my blood was thoroughly thinned by my residence down South, I dressed for the impending arctic conditions. Starting with thermals, I worked my way out to jeans and a woolly mammoth sweater in a lovely earth green, finishing with snow socks and boots. I pulled my hair back in its customary braid and brushed artificial roses to a bloom along my unremarkable cheekbones. When I could do no more, I collected coat, hat and gloves, and opened the door that separated my over-the-garage apartment-by-Goodwill from my sister's House Beautiful.

Though Rosemary and I started from the same fertilized egg, she is able to manage her assets better than me . . . with the notable exception of Dag Kenyon, scum bag of the universe and the husband who came, screwed her over and went.

Down in the kitchen I found my mother watching the Gulf War on CNN. I knew I would. Just like I knew her meticulously plucked brows would make that arc into her gray fringe when she saw my clothing choice.

"Slacks for church, Isabel?" My mother has the perfect voice for registering disapproval. It is light, smooth and cool, but with bite, like plain yogurt.

"It's cold and I'm allergic to frostbite." I bent to root through the refrigerator for pickles.

"You'll reek of pickle if you use your fingers like that. Reverend Hilliard particularly dislikes pickles."

Pickle jar in hand, I looked up in time to catch the matchmaking gleam in her eye. Surely she wasn't that desperate to remove the stain of singleness from my name?

What was I thinking? Of course she was that desperate. The only thing she wanted more than my marriage to a testosterone carrier was Rosemary's ex-husband castrated and forced to live the rest of his life as an impotent handyman for a women's sorority.

She's still got some work to do on the forgiveness thing.

"How could anyone hate pickles?" Holding her avid gaze with my limpid one, I deliberately submerged my hand in the jar, then wiped the pungent residue down the side of my jeans. If I had to, I'd hang dill around my neck to keep the reverend away. No way I was getting intimate with a guy that close to God.

"Maybe her tight jeans will distract him from the smell," my sister, Rosemary, said from the doorway, with a shadowed smile. Suffering agreed with her. Our mutual assets still looked better hanging from her bones than they ever had from mine.

"They are very tight," my mother began.

Luckily for me the telephone rang and dislocated the conversation. Before any of us could answer it, Rosemary's eldest daughter, Candice, swirled into the room and scooped up the receiver. Telephone answering is the only known benefit of having a thirteen-year-old in the house.

"Jeez, it's for you, Stan." She thrust the telephone at me like I'd committed a crime, then vanished like a comet, leaving a shimmering trail of hormones quivering in the air to mark her passage.

My mother stared at the place where Candice had been for a moment, then turned to look down her nose at me. "I wish you wouldn't encourage the children to call you Stan. Isabel is a lovely name."

No one needed encouragement to call me Stan, but I didn't waste breath pointing this out. I didn't have time for one of our automatic arguments. "Hello?"

"Isabel?"

No one except Muir Kenyon, that is. Muir would be at the top of my mother's potential husband list, purely because of his lukewarm interest in me, if he weren't also the brother of Rosemary's ex-husband. It's all very awkward but Muir is so clueless he hasn't figured that out yet.

"Hello, Muir."

"I was wondering if you would care to join me for a cup of hot chocolate this evening? I wrote a new computer program I'd like to show you." Muir's monotone droning in my ear barely registered until he mentioned chocolate.

Somehow Muir has realized I love hot chocolate like hobbits love mushrooms, while totally missing the fact that I find his computer programs terminally boring.

"Gee, I'm sorry, Muir. Reverend Hilliard asked me to play the organ for youth choir tonight."

"Well, that shouldn't last long. It's a school night, isn't it? Can we meet afterwards? I designed this program myself."

"I don't think so."

"I'll call you tomorrow then."

He would, too. It was depressing, but I didn't have time to

dwell on it. I had to leave before I compounded my sins by being late. I hung up the telephone and shrugged on my jacket, while surreptitiously examining Rosemary from under my lashes. She seemed to be in a fairly good mood.

"Could I borrow your Mercedes, Rose? My car was raised in New Orleans and doesn't know how to manufacture heat."

She frowned. Rosemary is a trifle possessive with her things. When we were kids in nursery school she used to spend the whole playtime with her toys stacked in the corner guarding them from forays by other kids. Time has not modified this tendency much. Added to the equation is my tendency to sometimes daydream while I drive, even occasionally ending up somewhere other than where I intended. Which doesn't mean I've put a scratch on anything of hers.

I watched her struggle between her protective passion for the car she'd wrested from her husband in the divorce settlement and the lowering knowledge she needed me to drive carpool in the morning because she had a class in glue gun technique.

"The keys are in my purse. Just be careful," she muttered.

"I'll treat it like it was my own."

Her brows shot up. "Not good enough."

"None of those accidents were my fault," I protested. "New Orleans is an automotive Bermuda Triangle!"

"One scratch—"

"Cross my heart and hope to die if I don't take care of your precious car." How lightly I said those words as I pulled on my wool fedora, tugging it down over my ears. How fate must have chortled with glee while my mother tsk-tsked and adjusted the hat to a more suitable angle on my head. When she was satisfied, she gave my cheek a pat that was partly fond, partly annoyed, and let me escape out the door for my rendezvous with destiny.

As soon as I was out of her sight, I jerked my hat down again. It was cold and I'm a grownup who can do what she likes when her mother isn't looking.

When the youthful hallelujahs faded into the frigid halls, I followed the hormonal herd to the kitchen for my earthly reward: the promised gourmet hot chocolate fix. At first the brew was too hot to drink, so I wrapped my hands around my cup, letting the warmth sink into my chilled fingers while I sniffed the fragrant, heavenly steam. After a time, I blew on the surface, took a tentative sip, then closed my eyes and savored the rich bouquet, the hint of hazel nut—

"Stanley!" Jerome Jeffries, youthfully oblivious to the finer nuances of hot chocolate consumption, pulled me to one side. "We got us a job!"

I guess this is where I admit I play keyboard and sing in a band. Lurking beneath my insignificant chest is a fairly impressive set of lungs, the better to fuel a decent set of vocal chords.

Jerome, cuter than Val Kilmer, a mere twenty years old, and the guiding light of the band, recruited me shortly after I moved home. It wasn't hard. I let myself be briefly dazzled with visions of jiving to "Wild Thing" or "I Love Rock'n Roll."

Very briefly.

Jerome had his sights set on becoming another Harry Connick, Jr. I thought we should call ourselves "Sad," but Jerome liked "Star Dust" better. So did my mother, who also pointed out that I was too old for such nonsense. I told her that actually I was too young.

For this reason, I greeted Jerome's announcement of a new gig with some wariness.

"Please tell me it's not another anniversary?" Anniversaries made my mother start digging up blind dates. Didn't matter to her that there were good reasons these guys were still single. Scary reasons.

"This is totally not an anniversary." His mouth curved into a grin that could have taught Tom Cruise a thing or two.

"It's a rally in support of the troops of Desert Storm at Grant Park! You won't believe this, but we've been asked to play back-up for the one and only Lee Greenwood!"

I waited a moment, but he didn't grin again.

"Lee Greenwood! Wow!" I paused. "Who's Lee Greenwood?"

Jerome laughed like I'd just been witty. Laughing kinked the area around his eyes, his mouth and my mid-section. I sipped my chocolate, the scientific equivalent of pouring gasoline on a fire and then tugged at the collar of my sweater. Perhaps the thermals were a mistake.

Tommy, our bass guitarist and a dead ringer for Michael J. Fox, mistook this for a summons and joined us. Okay, so it wasn't just the dream of playing in a band that made me agree to play bubble music on my weekends. I'm a Baptist, not a saint.

After more exclamations of mutual delight, we agreed to get together before the rally to rehearse. I downed the last of my chocolate as I watched them leave, almost reeling when the combined heat of their cute and my gourmet chocolate surged into my face, making my eyebrows sizzle and emit steam. Not content with sizzle, the heat spread out, seeking those parts of my body encased in thermal and wool. It was definitely time to get cool.

I headed for the door, but got cut off at the pass by Reverend Hilliard. I was starting to sweat buckets while the overhead lights put a halo around his cool blond hair. He smiled at me, two rows of gleaming, reverential teeth that nearly blinded me. He looked like he'd been born with the clerical collar around his neck.

I fought back a sudden urge to confess my recent lusting.

"I can't thank you enough for helping us out, Miss Stanley. I pray it didn't inconvenience you too much?"

He probably had prayed. Scary thought.

"It was no problem. I'm glad to help out the kids."

He smiled again, upping my guilt level dangerously.

I quickly added, "I really have to be going. I have Rosemary's car and she likes it home by ten."

He looked at me uncertainly. I took this for consent and fled. Outside the cold air sizzled against my hot cheeks. In another moment I'd spontaneously combust. I quickly stripped off the jacket, hat and gloves, tossing them into the back seat, then slid in and started the motor. The heater blew cold. Before it could change its mind, I switched it to cold vent and opened the sunroof, welcoming the combined rush of frigid air across my gently steaming face and neck.

Earlier, snow had mixed with rain. Clouds still obscured the stars, but the air was now dry and empty. In the fitful light of the street lamps, the road gleamed slick and empty. I drove cautiously, enjoying the feel of fresh air, sweet solitude—a rare commodity in our over-stocked household—and a great car to drive.

Pleasantly tired and full of chocolate, I drove on autopilot, my thoughts drifting to my current romance novel with its impending love scene that I still didn't know how to write.

"Get a better imagination or a lover, Stan," my agent had advised, the one time I'd let her read a draft.

"Maybe I should get a new agent," I muttered. About then I saw the stop sign and hit the brakes. Across the intersection, an unfamiliar street retreated into murk, lit only by the faint glow of the street lamps.

"Great." I'd done it again. I crossed the intersection, straining to read the signs. The names were vaguely familiar, but I couldn't place myself relative to home—

To my right, several firecrackers went off, one right after the other.

Then a man burst through the bay window of a house.

Chapter Two

At the sight of him, my mind switched to automatic stupor. With Orphan Annie eyes, I watched flying glass shards sparkling in the fitful light, a deadly rain showering the fast moving figure doing a movie stuntman roll across the ground. He sprang to his feet in a crouch, a cornered animal caught against the faint shimmer of wet grass.

More fireworks? No, shots!

Gunshots, I realized with numb horror. They spurted from the shattered window as the man darted for the street, his coat billowing out behind him like Count Dracula's cape.

Automatic reflex took my foot from gas to brake. On a subliminal level I knew I didn't want to drive into a shoot out. More shots. The man vaulted onto a car parked by the curb. I drew level, lost sight of him, then heard a thud. The car rocked.

What the—

Streetlight filtering down through the sunroof was abruptly blotted out. I looked up just in time to get a face full of him as he slid through the narrow sun roof head first, his entrance into the car hastened by my instinctive stomp on the brakes.

My mother had waited a long time for a man to fall into my lap, but I don't think this was what she had in mind.

Enveloped in his coat and buffeted by his knees, the muffled sound of gunshots came closer. I heard him shout, "Get us the hell out of here!"

Of course. Get out of here. I applied pressure to the gas. I should have waited until I could see.

We rocketed down the street. At least I hoped it was the street. Adrenaline kept pace with acceleration. I clawed at the coat over my face in literal blind panic, which gave way to clear-sighted panic when I emerged into light and air just in time to narrowly miss a parked Volvo.

The street looped in a U-turn. Rosemary's car didn't. We jolted up over the curb and passed through a neat, little hedge, winter-bare branches flying in all directions. A porch loomed into view.

A porch!

I cranked frantically on the wheel. The car bucked the turn. I knew why. My foot was on the gas. Knowing didn't help me lighten up. Grass and twigs sprayed in a graceful arc as the bushes that fronted the porch scraped the full length of Rosemary's car.

I wailed my dismay as the car blasted through the hedge on the other side of the yard, then lurched across the driveway in the narrow space between a parked station wagon and a tree.

Though concerned with my own plight, I was still aware of my unexpected passenger. Impossible not to be aware of him when he was using my nose as leverage for his foot. The other foot was still sticking out the sunroof. Part of his mid-section was draped over the gear shift severely hampering my efforts to steer around trees, garbage cans, and bicycles.

I heard him gasp when the car bounced down the curb. I really wanted to help him out—or off—but my brain wasn't getting through to my foot. Instead of slowing, the car picked up speed until the headlights illuminated a red stop sign.

Habit took over from there. At the sudden change in motion, the car shrieked in protest. My brain echoed the shriek when my head bounced off the steering wheel a couple of times. We slued left, then right. The ring of stars circling my head did the same, only opposite.

Car and stars stopped. The car was resting against the curb next to the stop sign. The stars settled into my head and became a crown of ouch.

My first feeling was relief.

I wasn't dead.

Rosemary's car was okay.

My passenger took his shoe out of my nose and climbed off the gear shift, bringing my attention back to the fact that I wasn't alone.

I was sharing car space with a man someone had been shooting at. Rosemary's passion for this car was directly related to how much her ex had hated to lose it in the divorce settlement, so retreat was not an option and I had no weapon.

I did take a self-defense course once. All I could remember was a distractingly cute instructor and something about defensive posture and making a lot of noise. I couldn't see how noise would help here, so I straightened my shoulders. It hurt.

"You all right?" he asked.

He didn't sound dangerous. Careful about what I moved because I don't do pain well, I looked at my sun-roof diver.

The light wasn't too bad to see him.

He wasn't too bad to look at.

Cute in a classy, upwardly mobile, dazed yuppie kind of way, I couldn't see his eyes because he was grimacing as he straightened his body into the standard, upright position in the seat. The nose between the eyes was straight and true in a cleanly sculpted face. The hair was good, both in cut and color. The streetlight found some blond highlights buried in brown and illuminated them to a pleasing glow.

He had to be at least six feet tall because he sat higher in the seat than me and I was five-nine in my stocking feet. His coat-covered shoulders filled all available space, while a heady male scent tightened my chest and turned my breathing almost languorous.

Practically a romance novel moment. Perhaps some mental note taking was in order, just in case I survived the encounter?

He sighed, relaxing the grim straightness of his mouth to a weary pout that warmed my insides like gourmet hot chocolate.

This was a dangerous man, possibly very dangerous, I realized with an un-Baptist-like thrill.

Unease quivered in the pit of my tum. I wasn't scared and I should be. I should be very scared.

"Get out." I sounded so firm I startled myself.

He brushed his hair back off the broad, proud expanse of his forehead, seemed surprised to find hand and head still there. With another grimace, he turned and showed me his eyes.

I wasn't ready for them. Or him. Every nerve ending in my body came to attention. I think some of them saluted. Was that a hallelujah chorus I heard? Some violins? No one, no *man* should be allowed to have eyes so round and spaced for maximum impact. Framed by curving, winged brows of sable and ridiculously long lashes.

Cool. Blue. Sounded tame, but his eyes weren't tame. They were wild, with the kind of cool that burned straight down to the quivering hearts and souls of innocents. He probably walked through life on broken hearts strewn in his path by virgins. Vestal and non-Vestal.

I didn't want to give him mine. I tried to look away.

I couldn't.

He pushed his hair back again. "Look, I'm sorry about this, but we've got to get away from here. Now."

His voice sent shivers down my spine. His words loosed a horde of questions in my head. Get away from what? Then I realized he was looking at me like I was the dangerous one.

He continued with an attractive urgency, "They'll come after us. I'd better drive. The odds are already against us."

"Really?" He wasn't that attractive. Outrage gathered my scattered senses from the four corners of my brain. "You'll drive this car when hell freezes—"

"Look, love." Without warning, he was in my space, his hands on my shoulders, his face so close I could see the smooth texture of his skin and smell him, not his after-shave. He smelled good. "There's no time. If they come after us . . . we go or we die."

Now, when it was too late, I felt the undercurrent beneath his yummy, civilized surface. The yuppie had a dark side and I was in his way. Fear spiked faster than lust. I went from hot to cold in the space of a single heartbeat.

"Don't hurt me. Please."

I hated how begging I sounded, but at least he quit gripping my shoulders. One hand drifted up to cup my cheek. Heat bloomed where he touched, sending impossible comfort to battle fear.

"Sweetheart, I'm trying to save you."

I dug deep, times like this it paid to be my mother's daughter, and probed his eyes again, this time looking for sincerity. He did sincere really good. I wanted, no, I needed to believe him. If his dark side was gonna mow me down, I didn't want to see it coming.

"What do you want me to do?" My dry whisper sounded

distant and kind of hollow.

His smile was relieved and as dangerous as bullets to one in my vulnerable state. The bastard had a dimple. I didn't whimper, but only because my throat was too dry.

"If you'll stand up, I'll slide under you—"

Slide? Surely he wasn't planning to scale the gear shift again?

"You're kidding. Aren't you?" His brows arched in an unspoken query. Suddenly I was on the same page he was. The one where neither of us trusted the other one enough to get out of the car.

"I'll just—" I looked up, then reached up and hooked my fingers over the open edge of the sunroof. His hands, warm and strong, went around my waist, providing extra boost.

"Can you pull your legs clear?" he asked.

I tried to concentrate, but it wasn't easy. I worked my legs clear of the steering wheel. With only minimal skin loss, I got one foot on the armrest attached to the door, the other on the steering wheel and pulled until my head emerged into crisp night air. But gravity was already sending out an insistent summons that was getting harder and harder to ignore. Sweaty palms weren't helping me either.

I heard a shrill woof. What now?

An excitable dust mop dog was doing a "job" on the corner lawn. At the other end of his leash was an old man staring at me with shocked pleasure. I didn't want to, but it was no use. Like Orpheus, I was descending. I caught my passenger just as he was mounting the gear shift.

I'll never forget the sound he made.

Or the whimper he gave when I crawled off him and onto the passenger seat. Moving like an old man, he finished his descent into the driving position. I opened my mouth to apologize, saw a minivan careen around the corner in an ominous manner and turned the apology into a warning wail of dismay.

Apparently warning wail was a language he was familiar with. In a heartbeat, he shook off the blow to his male pride, put the car in gear and hit the gas. We accelerated with a squeal that left me open-mouthed.

Behind us the minivan miscreants opened fire. The bullets thudded into Rosemary's car. Fear thudded into my heart. Why, oh why had I crossed my heart and hoped to die? I was so far up the creek, I should just beat myself to death with the paddle and be done with it. If the minivan shooter didn't plug me, Rosemary would. With her glue gun.

We sped through the quiet neighborhood, the street lights blurring to a ribbon of gold in our wake. Corners were taken on two wheels.

I turned to protest his wanton car abuse, but when I looked at him protest dried up in my throat. My heart pounded with fright and a complicated longing to be someone daring enough to go with the moment. And with the man. I was the only component that didn't fit. Questions rose, like tiny bubbles breaking on the surface of my mind. I even opened my mouth to ask him. . . .

And snapped it closed again. In books and the movies, knowing what was going on was a Bad Thing. Of course, so was speeding through the suburbs at a million miles an hour.

A straight stretch of road let him give me a quick, assessing glance. I pointedly buckled my seat belt.

"Look, Mr.—"

"Kapone. Kelvin Kapone."

"Ca—" I swallowed dryly, "—pone?"

"Ka-pone," he corrected, "with a 'K' No relation to Al."

I managed a weak laugh. "Of course not."

Just because we were being chased through a subdivision

by armed maniacs in a minivan was no reason to assume it was because his name was Ka-pone.

He made a quick turn, the rear wheels shrieking across the pavement, a short burst forward, then another turn onto a long, straight street that paralleled the park I walk my dog in. It was strangely comforting to find myself in familiar territory.

The car suddenly slowed and I looked at Kelvin Kapone-with-a-K in alarm. "What's wrong?"

"Nothing." His gaze roved between the road ahead and the rear view reflection of the minivan.

"We're slowing down. They'll catch up with us." I tried not to sound shrill, but I don't think I succeeded.

"I know. I'm gonna force them off the road."

"How—" But I already knew. I'd seen the movies with their disposable Hollywood cars. "Not with my sister's car!"

As if I hadn't spoken, he eased Rosemary's car into the center lane. The minivan jumped like a dog smelling blood and swung over to my side. I was caught in a waking, slow motion nightmare. Frozen in horror, I stared in the side mirror at the steadily gaining minivan.

Then I didn't need the mirror. Fake wood veneer trim and pea green paint pulled into my peripheral vision. Above the veneer an open window framed the driver.

He had a gun.

It was pointed at me.

Behind the round, dark barrel was a shadowy figure with a round, hairless head, round mouth and round eyes. I tried to become one with my seat as Rosemary's car began to veer toward the van.

I don't remember lunging for the wheel, just found my hands around it. I jerked it. We careened across the street and up the curb into the park. He yelled as he fought the skid across the winter brown grass of the park. A metal skeleton rose like a ghost in the night. A jungle gym set. Kelvin yelled again. Something that might have been obscene. I yelled, too. Something definitely obscene.

He pulled madly on the wheel. I pressed feet against a brake I wished I had. We missed the jungle gym by inches and skidded through the uprights of a swing set. The rubber swings scraped across the roof, banging briefly in the open top. I don't know how he managed to avoid wrapping the car around the supports.

He looked dazed. "Can we get back to the street this way?"

"Yes," I gasped, "just past the airplane—"

"Airplane?" The headlights grazed the edge of it.

"Mem-or-i-al—" The word bounced with the car as we crossed a lumpy area in the grass. Something to do with earthworms, according to my mother. Bounce turned into a skid. Kelvin straightened the car and looked at me.

I looked back, thought I saw something square and gray in the grass. "What was that?"

"I think it was cement."

"Cement?" The headlights of the minivan bobbed in our wake, then went side ways as it hit the patch. We descended to the street with a neck wrenching lurch, then he punched it, throwing me back against the seat as the car surged forward.

"Time to lose those clowns."

We had a slight lead and he took advantage of it, executing a series of lightning, frightening turns that finished in a dark driveway. He pulled deep into the shadows beneath a stand of trees and shut off the engine. Something wet landed on me. I looked up. The sunroof was still open and it was snowing again. Through the opening, there came the unmistakable sound of an approaching vehicle.

"Is it—them?" I huddled down in the seat. Let the elements come as long as the bad guys didn't.

"Maybe."

What, he couldn't trot out a comforting lie?

His arm brushed against mine, his clothes rustling. He pulled something from inside his coat, something that gleamed dull and dangerous in the deep darkness. He held it up and checked the cartridge, slid it back into the base, loaded a bullet into the chamber, then settled back in the seat, his face turned toward the street.

A sheen of sweat gave definition to the determined angle of his jaw. His eyes glimmered with a deadly light that was comforting until a tremor passed like quicksilver along his jaw. He swallowed and shook his head, then rubbed his eyes like they hurt him. Or he couldn't see.

A glacier of fear formed along my spine. The hand holding the gun quivered, then started to shake. He rubbed his face. The van slowly idled closer to our hiding place. He shuddered, his body hunching over as if in pain. "Sorry—"

He slumped against the door.

The hand holding the gun went slack.

The thunk of it against the floor coincided perfectly with the arrival of the van at the foot of the driveway.

Chapter Three

My life started to flash before my eyes, but right away I got bogged down coming up with explanations for some things that God might not understand. Above the frantic thump of my heart I heard the hum of an engine. The metallic creak of an opening door was followed by the scrape of cowboy boots against pavement.

I abandoned explanations and went for the gun.

As I groped across his unconscious body, snowflakes drifted down, settling on my exposed neck like tiny, icy fingers that quickly turned into rivulets trickling down my back. Fear made a knot in my stomach above the spot the gear shift was digging into.

If I got out of this alive, I wasn't driving manual again.

It took me a moment to register wet warmth against my face. A sickly sweet smell. Even before I lifted my head for a look, I knew what I'd find. He wasn't the type to pass out from fright.

Blood. He was bleeding—

The sudden blast of light was startling, painful even after the near black I'd been straining to peer through. Had a heavenly apparition appeared to save me?

Only if the angel was disguised as a skinny, bald guy in a bathrobe holding a shotgun. He peered into the dark outside his stoop, his hands working the firing mechanism. Cowboy boots didn't linger to see if the bald guy was serious. He just scuttled back down the driveway.

I didn't have time to enjoy relief that the old guy didn't see us parked deep in the shadows behind his Jeep. My companion was bleeding to death all over my sister's car. Despite a deficiency in my Florence Nightingale gene and because it was tradition, I mentally ran down the list of what I was wearing that could be converted into a bandage.

Bra was out. Dispensable, but minuscule. Non-absorbent sweater. That left my thermals. I eyed him suspiciously before turning my back to him and shedding the woolly sweater, then the thermal top. Between the chill of the night air on my nearly bare upper body and fear, my teeth were chattering up a storm before I got my sweater back on and turned toward my patient.

It didn't take long to apply the starkly white thermals to his manly, bloody chest. I had to use my chin to hold the top in place while I shoved both my arms and its sleeves behind his back and knotted the sleeves.

Despite the seriousness of the situation, I felt ridiculous crouched over the gear shift, chin deep in blood, hugging an unconscious man so I could knot my underwear around his mid-section.

Unfortunately he started to stir while my arms were still wrapped around him. I opened my mouth to babble an explanation, but only managed a squeak before he reciprocated the wrapping of arms and upped the stakes by nuzzling my neck with his mouth.

I would have struggled, but I was so shocked. Then, well, the feel of his mouth on my skin, his warm breath stirring the tendrils of my hair felt—good. Besides, if I struggled it might loosen the makeshift bandage. Not struggling was the righteous thing to do.

It was darn near noble.

And good for my career as a romance writer. You just couldn't buy this kind of experience. At least, I didn't think so.

"Ummmm," he murmured, the pleasure sound came from deep in his throat, "you taste good."

"Really?" Trembling heat from his mouth tangled with trailing chills from the snowflakes drifting through the sunroof onto my exposed neck. It would have been better without the gear shift digging into my bladder, but sin had a price tag.

Sweet sin.

He found a particularly sensitive spot just under my ear and proceeded to nibble there, temporarily overpowering the effect of the flakes and the gear shift. My bones dissolved, like an Alka-Seltzer in water, swirling around, tickling my insides with aching pleasure. His mouth moved higher, tasting and tantalizing, on a collision course with my unfortunately eager mouth. I pursed my lips in preparation—

Instead of lip locking, he looked up, taking away the warm and letting the chill back in.

I un-pursed my lips and looked up, too. A fat, wet snowflake landed in my eye.

"It's snowing." His voice was a husky murmur, setting off a landslide of shivers along my spine.

"No kidding." I blinked away the blur. He was quiet, but I could hear his mental wheels starting to crank up again. This seemed a good time to deny complicity in the embrace. "Could you let me go? The gear shift is giving me another navel."

His hands fell away. "What—"

Back in my cold seat, I shifted uncomfortably. "I was just trying to bandage your wound and you got . . . confused."

Incredibly, he produced a slight smile. "What happened to the van?"

"Oh. They left. This bald guy in a bathrobe scared them off with a shotgun."

"I see." He didn't sound like he did, but that didn't stop him from reaching for the keys. "Let's get out of here."

I covered his hand.

"This time I drive," I said. "I'm more likely to stay conscious." We traded places the usual way, though the walk around the car cost him. He faded out on me before I got the car started. When I backed out of the driveway I saw a police cruiser turn the corner ahead of us, which probably explained why the minivan was no where in sight. That didn't stop me from checking all possible directions during the endless drive to the hospital. I was so busy checking, I missed my turn and had to backtrack to the hospital from a different direction. Even then I almost didn't see the minivan lurking in the shadows near the emergency room door. Luckily it was facing the wrong way to see us.

I don't know how they knew that he'd been injured, possibly he'd left a blood trail in the house. I just knew we'd never make it inside those doors. And even if we did, anyone who watched TV knew how dangerous a hospital is to someone being stalked by killers. That left my vet, who might be better than a doctor, since they learned to doctor lots of species, not just one. At least that's what I told myself.

I met Mike Lang when I adopted Addison over the stringent objections of my mother. She doesn't like anything that licks its butt or smells hers. Mike doesn't seem to mind either of these things. He's easy going and kind of like his doggy patients, large and shaggy with dark eyes, a slow, deep voice and endless patience.

He needed that patience when he got me and my dog. Not only is Addison my first dog, but I have this habit of picking up and bringing Mike wounded strays. Though I've never brought him one this late before. Or this particular breed.

He probably shouldn't have attached his practice to his house. It's just too easy to find him.

The heat from my passenger's nibbling had faded, leaving me feeling cold and wobbly when I scrambled out of the car. I retrieved my jacket from the back seat and pulled it on for the walk to Mike's door. After pressing the bell, I sagged against the door frame and took a brief nap.

"Stan?"

I opened my eyes to find Mike towering over me, his hairy legs planted like twin tree trunks. He was wearing an elegant robe that opened to expose dark, curling chest hair all the way to his navel.

I averted my gaze from the vee because I was already in a very weakened condition.

"Do you know what time it is?"

"Time?" I shook my head, feeling a strange detachment. "No."

Mike's eyes narrowed sharply and he grabbed my chin, turning my face towards the mellow porch light. He rubbed a thumb lightly across my temple, then examined the dark smudge it had acquired.

I looked at it, too.

"Blood? What the hell's going on? Is Addison hurt?"

"No—" I hesitated, not quite sure how to broach the subject of whose blood it was.

He sighed hugely, almost breaching the fragile closure of his robe. I'd never noticed what a nice chest he had. Course I'd never seen it uncovered until now.

"If you don't stay away from strays, you're going to get hurt."

"No kidding."

"Where is this stray of yours?"

"In Rosemary's car. Though there's something I should mention—"

He was already moving away, his long legs using up the distance between his door and Rosemary's car far too quickly. I trotted after him like an apologetic mongrel.

"I just hope it's not rabid this time." Mike bent and grabbed the door handle.

"No, but . . ."

The door came open, the interior light throwing a ghastly glow on the man slumped in the seat. His dark coat and darker suit jacket fell open, giving us a first-class view of my formerly white underwear bandage and his formerly white shirt. Scarlet trails dripped from his limp hand onto the concrete between Mike's feet.

"I can't believe I let you talk me into this!" Mike's face was uncharacteristically grim as he eased Kelvin Kapone-with-a-K onto the examining table.

"I'm sorry, Mike, but I couldn't take him to the hospital in this condition! They'd have killed him!"

Mike looked at me for a moment. Opened, then closed his mouth, clearly struck dumb by my masterful logic. I guess, I decided with a spurt of pride, I wasn't as tired as I felt.

He switched on the harsh, overhead light and turned to his new patient. Since this was my first opportunity to see my passenger in good light, I turned toward him, too. I half expected to be disappointed, but even with the color gone from his face and his chest covered in blood, he didn't disappoint. Broad shoulders, lean hips, good bones and taut flesh, all nicely packaged.

His hair was more blond than I'd thought, his skin lightly tanned, as if he'd just come back from a sunny climate. His mouth—I realized I was rubbing my neck where his mouth had been and quickly pulled my hand down. What kind of Baptist checks out an unconscious man?

My mother had raised me to be Fundamental, not elemental.

Mike laid bare the wound. He looked up, his face grim. "This is a bullet wound."

"Really?" I tried to look surprised.

"You're telling me you didn't know?"

I avoided his gaze. "I didn't see him get shot. I just saw people shooting at him."

"Oh! And that makes a difference?"

"No." I shook my head, feeling an attack of the profounds coming on, but I was in no condition to stop it. "Life is just too weird. I mean, little tiny things, like a simple phone call can just send your life spinning right off the track."

"What?"

I stared at him owlishly. "Do you know that if Mrs. MacPhearson hadn't gotten the flu, we'd both be snug in bed right now and . . ." And I would never have met Kelvin Kapone-with-a-K. Funny how that seemed worse than getting shot at.

Mike's expression lightened. "Snug in bed . . . together?"

I gave him the Look. "Why do men have to be so male?"

"Even the boyfriend?"

"He's not my boyfriend." Darn it.

He looked pleased. "So what is he?"

"What is he?" I opened my eyes and my mouth, hesitated, and then shrugged, trying to act casual. "He's Kelvin . . ." It didn't seem wise to mention the Kapone-with-a-K part. Mike would probably have the same reaction to the name I'd had. ". . . my friend. Kelvin. That's who he is. My friend . . ."

". . . Kelvin," Mike finished, looking suspicious. I didn't blame him.

"Yes. Kelvin. My friend."

I smiled innocently, then turned and picked up the bloody suit jacket Mike had tossed on the floor. The fine dark wool was as soft as baby skin and gave off a faint whiff of something exotic, as if it routinely went places I could only dream about.

"Do you really know this guy?"

"I don't know him *well.*" I felt as defensive as if he were my mother. "It's just that, well, I met him recently, after choir practice actually. Church choir practice."

When being deceptive, it's better to be truthfully deceptive.

I gave the coat a hearty shake, releasing a tiny shower of white cards. Business cards? I knelt down, swept them into a tidy pile and gathered them up.

"So what does this guy do, when he's not getting shot?"

The cards fanned across my hand. They all bore the name Kelvin Kapone. It really was with a "K." But each card seemed to be for a different business or job. Import-export, travel agent, engineer—

"Portable toilet sales?" I let the words out involuntarily. In the corner was a sketch of a little tiny outhouse. "Potties-Are-Us?"

Mike looked surprised, then pleased. Maybe it was a guy thing, a vet being higher on the pecking order than a toilet salesman. I shoved the cards back in the pocket, folded the jacket and lay it across a metal chair, my gaze returning to the man lying still on the table.

It didn't take that many brain cells to know the one thing he wasn't was a portable toilet salesman. Whatever I'd gotten mixed up in, it had nothing to do with bodily function. At least not that kind.

He was pale. A piece of his hair had fallen forward and now curled, appropriately enough, into a question mark. I wanted to smooth it back and take his hand, but I didn't have the right or the necessary nerve.

"Is he going to be all right?"

"It looks worse than it is. The bullet just raked the surface of the ribs." Mike was quiet for a moment, then burst out, "I can't believe I'm saying this so calmly! This man was shot!"

"I know, I can't believe it either." If we'd made it into the hospital, I'd be trying to explain all this to a policeman and I didn't have a clue what all this was about. And now I'd involved Mike, too. "I suppose you have, like some hypocritical oath to report this?"

"Vet's don't take the Hippocratic oath, but I do have to file a report if he has rabies."

"Ha, ha." I gave him a haughty look.

"We're both culpable if we don't report a crime!"

"I know that. I just think he should report his own crime. He knows more about it than I do. I'm Jane Innocent Bystander here!"

Mike stared at me, then gave another one of those robe popping sighs, but he was behind the table so I didn't have to avert my gaze.

"Then I'd better get him fixed, hadn't I?"

I couldn't help myself. "Fixed? Isn't that a little drastic?"

"Why don't you go do something?" He tried to sound annoyed, but I could see the twinkle creep back into his eyes.

"Like mop up Rosemary's car?"

"Please."

There was a flashlight in the glove compartment. It even worked. I used it to give the outside of the car a once over. It was easy to see the scratches in the dusty surface of the car, impossible to tell if they went through to the paint. I found at least one bullet hole, low on the right side, just above the bumper. I knew there had to be one, maybe two more.

Inside, it was even harder to assess the damage. The upholstery was dark, so how was I supposed to tell which spots were snow water and which were blood?

It was cold, frigid actually, and my hands were getting numb. I pushed the seat forward and scrabbled around until I found my hat and gloves on the floor on top of my purse. My purse? I hadn't brought my purse, just shoved my driver's license into my pocket.

I bent to push the purse under the seat. It was an open invitation for theft and I didn't need to have a smashed window added to my list of car crimes. But when my hand slid across the cheap plastic surface, I hesitated. Rosemary had traded up from plastic years ago. And it was too maroon and small to be my mother's. On one side was a jagged tear.

I undid the clasp. There was no ID inside, just a shopping list and some coupons, an invitation to a meeting for something called PT-PAC, a typewriter claim ticket issued by Kenyon Business Machines, my ex-in-laws' company, and a matchbook from the Tandoor Club, which claimed to specialize in Moroccan cuisine and exotic dancers.

I turned the matchbook over and studied the cartoon belly dancer on the front. A strange thing to find nestled next to a coupon for adult diapers.

"Stan?" I looked up to see Mike beckoning to me from the doorway and hurriedly stuffed the things back into the purse, then shoved it under the seat. It was time to see about my patient. The mystery of the purse could be solved later.

Chapter Four

Back in Mike's examining room, our patient was sitting up and sporting a neat bandage across his chest in place of the bloodied shirt. I examined bandage and chest.

"Very nice." I caught Mike watching me watch our patient, who was watching me. Caught between gazes I couldn't comfortably meet, I changed mine to a poster of a dog skeleton on the wall. "You're awake."

You're good, Stan. Truly inspired.

"Yeah." I heard the grin in his voice and had to see the dimple again. It was as good as I remembered. Added to his potent blue gaze, I forgot I was too tall, too flat-chested, my makeup long gone and probably still sporting his blood.

"Do you know how much you weigh?" Mike asked, breaking into the strange intimacy of the moment.

We both looked at Mike. Good thing he wasn't looking at me, because I wasn't about to share my weight any time soon.

Kelvin shrugged. "About one-eighty, maybe. Why?"

"I want to give you a couple of shots, antibiotic and some painkiller. You're going to be a little sore for a few days." Mike held up a tiny bottle, drawing the liquid from it up into a syringe. He hesitated, the needle still imbedded in the bottle, and looked at me. "Do you remember what Addison weighed last time you brought him in?"

"Last time I brought him in he wouldn't sit on the scales."

"Oh. Yeah. He sat on me." He frowned.

"Who's Addison?" our patient asked, with understandable confusion.

"Addison is my dog."

Comprehension didn't dawn in his blue eyes, but I stared into them a bit longer, just to be sure. Mike squirted a little fluid from the end of the long needle.

"You're not a fainter, are you?"

Kelvin seemed fascinated by the glistening length of steel. "I don't think so."

Mike swabbed Kelvin's arm. "Had this three hundred pound jock pass out on my desk just because the prof stuck a needle in a grapefruit. Broke my wrist." He jabbed the needle into flesh.

Kelvin winced and stared fixedly at the poster of the dog skeleton. When he'd delivered both doses, Mike tossed the syringes, pulled a couple of packets of tablets out of a drawer and handed them to him.

"Here's some painkiller and another dose of antibiotic for the morning. It should hold you until you can get to your regular doctor. The dosage is iffy, so only take one of the pain pills at a time and only if you need it."

Kelvin held the packet up. "Kind of big to swallow, doc."

"You don't swallow them. You crush them and sprinkle them on your feed—" Mike stopped. "Or your breakfast. You could sprinkle them on your breakfast cereal."

Kelvin's face was carefully blank, his eyes a couple of blue mirrors. "You're not a people doctor, are you?"

Mike looked at me.

"What?" I looked at Kelvin, ready to explain, but hoping I wouldn't have to in front of Mike. Kelvin didn't ask for an explanation, but I didn't feel relieved. The lack of expression on his face was unnerving.

Mike got Kelvin a shirt that almost swallowed him whole,

but failed to make him look ridiculous or less dangerous.

"Take it easy," Mike cautioned, "and don't be surprised if the medication makes you a little sleepy."

Mike walked with us out to the car, stood with his hands in the pockets of his robe, his feet bare despite snow still drifting down.

Kelvin gritted his teeth and sank onto the seat. "Thanks for your help, doc."

Mike nodded, shut the door and turned to me. "You sure he's not your boyfriend?"

"Quite sure," I said, surprised he'd even asked. "How much do I owe you?"

He scratched his beard with a massive hand, looking toward the cloudy sky. A few snowflakes lodged in the dark hair. "How about dinner and a movie?"

"With me?"

Mike grinned. "I think I've spent enough time with him."

I smiled back, despite a slight qualm at getting a date out of Kelvin's misfortune. One way or another, it had been quite a night.

"Okay."

"Tomorrow. At seven?"

I frowned. "Better make it eight. Rosemary's club is having a wax fruit retrospective until seven thirty."

"Wax fruit?"

"According to my mother it makes more sense than writing my cockroach books."

Mike laughed softly, the vee of his robe gaping provocatively as his big chest shook. "You're certainly full of surprises, Miss Stanley."

I fingered the rich brocade of his lapel, as surprised at myself as he was. Maybe it had to do with almost getting wasted. "So are you, Dr. Lang. I'll see you tomorrow."

I inserted myself into the car for the final lap of my adventure. As I pulled away, I think the wind caught the flap of Mike's robe but I was too much of a lady to look. It was too dark to see anything anyway.

"Care to explain why I was patched by a dog doctor?"

I gave him a wary look. "The hospital didn't seem like a good idea with your gun-toting friends lurking outside. They beat us to the Emergency Room."

"Well, well, isn't that interesting."

Interesting? That people wanted to kill him bad enough to stake out a hospital? What had I gotten myself involved in? I stopped at a red light and looked at him. I was eager, despite his obvious assets, to get uninvolved *poste* haste. It was decision and directions time. I cleared my throat. He didn't respond.

"Hello? Where do you go from here?"

He turned his head slowly, like he was afraid it would fall off. Then he blinked twice. "Why are you . . . spinning?"

"I'm not spinning."

"Am I spinning?"

"No." He slumped heavily against my shoulder. "Great. Might make him a little sleepy, Mike?" I rubbed my face. "Now what am I supposed to do?"

I looked down at him. His lashes fanned across his cheek, his mouth curved in a slight pout, and his deep, even breathing ruffled the hair next to my ear. What is it that we women find so appealing about a little-boy-lost quality when we know exactly what little boys are made of? And how do we get over it?

When I pulled Rosemary's car into its slot in her garage, my uninvited guest didn't stir from his position against my side. All the way home his body lying against mine had taken away the chill and replaced it with feelings I thought I'd safely stowed in the hope-less chest my mother had insisted on buying for me in the season of her hope.

I didn't waste time dwelling on what his reaction would be when he came to in the morning, focusing instead on the logistical problems of actually getting him out of the car and into my apartment. The problem with an over-the-garage apartment is that it is over the garage.

"Mr. Kapone?"

No response.

"Wouldn't you like to go to bed? I know I would."

"Bed?" he murmured, stirring slightly. A faint, reminiscent smile curved his mouth.

"Brings back pleasant memories, does it?" It seemed I'd found the magic word. I scrambled out and went round to his door. "Time to come to bed."

It worked better than Pavlov's dog bell. He turned toward me, his lashes at half mast, lifting his feet clear of the car and lowering them to the floor like it was a moving surface. Maybe from his perspective it was.

I took his hands, ignored a mental click as they fit together, braced myself and pulled. He came up eagerly, if groggily, so eagerly we staggered into my mother's van occupying the other slot. I slid my arms around him to steady him. I don't know why he slid his arms around me. His eyes, though hazy and unfocused, still managed to be unsettling.

"Do you think you can make it up the stairs?"

Instead of answering, he smiled.

Some men were born to smile at women. He was one of those men. It was an arrow shot straight through the armor of my resolve. If my toes hadn't curled into hooks, he would have knocked my socks off.

He smoothed the escaped hair off my face, the sweetly abrasive palm of his hand brushing against my skin in the process. When the hand settled in for a visit, I realized I might be in trouble. When my breathing changed into this gaspy, CPR-like rhythm, I knew I was in trouble. How could I have known the delights of the flesh were this, well, delightful?

His head bent towards mine, setting off a chain reaction in my mid-section. My insides curled like a ribbon when you run scissors along it. The blood in my face went all tidal, creating a serious impediment to clear thought.

"Mr. Kapone—"

"Call me Kel," he murmured against my lips.

My lips really liked being murmured against. I licked them in anticipation and was rewarded with contact.

Sweet, sweet contact. Cold at first, but warming up fast. His hard, strong body lay against mine sending the rational part of my brain sliding down a spiral tunnel of delight.

He broke contact, despite an involuntary protest from moi, then made up for it by taking nibbling bites down the side of my neck. I arched up on my toes to give him easier access and realized I was gripping his shoulders. My hands slid down to his chest where his heart pounded a pagan siren's song into my palms, though I wasn't so far gone that I let them wander into the injury zone.

I'd already gone further than this Baptist had gone before.

"No wonder people wrote operas about love," I murmured, while tipping my head to allow access to a neglected spot clamoring for its turn.

His hands, warm and strong, kneaded my back, then slid down to cup my posterior, lifting me deep enough into his embrace to seriously assess his level of involvement. It was pretty high.

Even while my body quivered its delight, my brain was wondering how he could be drugged to the eyeballs and ready to jump my bones. I didn't dwell on why I was tempted to let him.

"Uh, excuse me?" I shifted my grip to the side of his head and pushed until I was looking in foggy blue eyes. "You're wounded. You need to lie down. You know, go to bed."

I knew right away I shouldn't have used the b-word.

His lids dropped to half mast. His nostrils flared. His mouth curved in sensuous anticipation. I tried to get my elbows between us, but he moved pretty fast for a drugged guy.

"Bed," he agreed, thickly, pulling me back into the hard cradle of his body and claiming my mouth with a deep hunger that filled a need I didn't know I had.

We started to slide sideways and the door handle of my mother's van dug into my back, a pointed reminder that I was going somewhere I'd never been with someone I didn't know. And doing it leaning against my mother's vehicle. Not good. I pulled my head away, and took several deep breaths.

"Please stop, I need . . ."

". . . to call me Kel." His mouth explored the right side of my face.

"Oh, my. . . ."

"Say it," he insisted, his dimple flirting at the edge of my vision. "Call me Kel."

"Oh, what the hell." Hadn't I just been mourning my love scene writing capabilities? Didn't I need some experience if I was ever to move past my roach? This was research, not sin. My arms slid back around him as my mouth sighed into his. "Kel."

Capitulation took the starch right out of me.

He retained his starch. It may even have gotten stiffer.

Our lips fused in a scorching contact that carried away sober Baptist and left hot-to-trot Gumby. When we came up for air, I made another weak protest, "You need to get to bed."

"Bed," he agreed, turning us both in the direction of the stairs. With many wobbles and bumps, and me removing his hand from my rump every other step, we made it. I even managed to get the key in the lock before he sprawled us across the door jamb onto the floor. Addison galloped up and licked Kel.

Kel rubbed his face. "What was that?"

"My dog. So behave yourself." I gave Addison a hearty thump on the head, then said, "Crate, Addison."

With a huge woof, Addison actually padded back to his crate.

"Good dog!" This was a night of many firsts.

I slipped out of my coat and tossed it over a chair, then helped Kel with his. He was swaying again, so I put my arm around his waist and steered him into my virginal bedroom.

I didn't have a hand free to find the light, so I made my best guess where the bed was, which turned out not be that good. I caught the bed with the back of my legs and went down, bringing him with me.

Kel didn't flinch, probably because of Mike's doggy painkiller. He even smiled before he kissed me again.

I sighed, too weary to fight him and my longings. His tongue found the breach in my lips and slipped in, an erotic caress that left my whole body limp with longing. Feeling instead of thinking, my hands slid into his hair and helped his mouth continue to wreak heady havoc on mine. I swear, the bed started to spin, with my heart going counter-clock-wise. I heard a moan and hoped it wasn't me. I tried to keep my eyes open, but all I saw was him, all I felt was him.

Then his hands, which had been busy while I was expanding my understanding of the male physique, found an opening in my clothing. The feel of his hands sliding up the bare skin of my stomach toward my breasts ignited fear and longing.

Caught between both, I couldn't move.

I teetered on the edge of giving in to pleasure, to crossing that threshold of knowing, of plunging into the secret world where male met female—when he stopped.

Not just stopped, he went totally limp.

From heady lover to Raggedy Andy in a heart beat. Doggie painkiller takes down passion. I tried to oust regret and replace it with the more proper relief. It would have been easier if he had rolled off me, since my nerve endings were still sparking with delight.

"Kel?"

He didn't move.

"Great." I pushed. He muttered and buried his face deeper against my neck. Even unconscious he felt really good.

It was too much. I was too tired to fight against the comfort of a warm, male embrace on a cold night. I'd just rest a minute, let him get really asleep, then I could slip away and curl up all alone on the cold, short, uncomfortable, couch.

Chapter Five

I was thirteen years old, when Freddie Frinker, the minister's son, gave me my first kiss on the front porch of my house the night of the Sadie Hawkins dance. It was squishy and slimy with too much tongue and too little yum. But the worse part was when he pulled back and I discovered we were still tenuously connected by a little strand of spit. With a tiny rainbow quivering at the center.

It was a watershed event in my life. I've had other embarrassing moments, but nothing that surpassed the horror of making a spit rainbow with Freddie Frinker.

That is, until I woke up in my bed wrapped around Kelvin Kapone with a "K." That he was wrapped around me did nothing to ease the situation. My head ached and I had the uneasy feeling that the kiss I'd been dreaming about hadn't been a dream at all. In a moment of mutual consent we moved apart. My move rolled me off the bed. The thump against the floor rattled the windows.

I cleared the huskiness from my throat and watched him from under my lashes as I said in my teacher's voice, "Good morning."

The corner of his mouth quivered once, but his eyes were as grave as his voice. "Good morning."

The silence stretched like Spandex until I produced my next inane remark. "How are you feeling?"

"Like I lost an argument with a truck." He gave a half grimace, half grin and pulled himself into a sitting position against the headboard.

At some point in the night he'd shed Mike's tent-like shirt. His bare chest, crossed by bandages and a sprinkling of blondish-brown hair, immediately improved the plain expanse of my headboard. He was still pale, with the faint shadow of a beard adding an attractive texture to his strong chin.

"Um, would you like one of the pain pills Mike gave you?"

"I don't think that would be a good idea, do you?" His voice was serious but his eyes, brightened by a highly suspect humor, met mine for a long moment.

He couldn't remember what happened last night, could he? I wanted to gnaw on this thought, the same way an animal will gnaw a limb caught in a trap, but it was hard to concentrate when he was examining my bedroom. How could he not notice it was a place where not much happened?

Plain, white walls and spare, natural wood furniture. The bed, though deep and soft, draped in prim white, except for the hideous purple afghan my mother had crocheted for me from some used yarn she'd picked up at a yard sale. I have many other even more hideous things she's made for me hidden in the hope-less chest at the foot of the bed. He kept his conclusions hidden behind a deliberately bland expression when he looked at me.

"I'm sorry I flaked out on you. Uh," he looked rueful, "do I know your name?"

"I don't think we got that far." I climbed awkwardly to my feet, feeling terribly morning after-ish despite being fully clothed. It didn't help that he seemed more comfortable in my bedroom than I did. I stuck out my hand. "Isabel Stanley, but everybody calls me Stan."

He took it, grip and shake firm. "Why?"

If he didn't know, I wasn't going to tell him.

"Why don't you go first in the shower?" I suggested.

He shook his head. "I'm still feeling a bit groggy and you probably have somewhere to go?"

I wanted to tell him he had somewhere to go, too, like out of my apartment before my mother saw him.

"I guess you probably shouldn't get your bandages wet."

"I'll think of something."

Why did I get the feeling he'd had this problem before?

Inside the bathroom, I avoided looking in the mirror as I undressed and climbed in the shower. Water flooded my body, relaxing it for two seconds. Only when I was thoroughly wet did I realize my clothes were out there with him. I cussed silently, pulled on my minuscule bathrobe, made sure it was securely fastened, took a deep breath and opened the door.

Kel was leaning against the frame of the French door that opened onto a little balcony that overlooked Rosemary's garden. I'd never be able to come in here again without remembering the way he looked against my white curtains with the winter-bare trees in the background. Or lay in my bed without remembering how it felt to be touched by a master craftsman.

He turned, managing to look both relaxed and alert, his brows arching over eyes openly amused. "I must be losing my touch."

"Huh?"

"When I spend the night with a woman—"

Was that admiration in the bold gaze sliding down my body? Heat followed the path of his eyes. The robe seemed too much to have on.

"—she usually undresses before we go to bed. Not after."

My throat went bone dry.

"Really?" I sounded indifferent, but had a feeling a rampaging blush gave me away. "How nice for you. I'll just see what I can do in the way of food while you wash up, Mr. Kapone."

I turned, the short distance to the door taking an eternity, when I could feel him watching me. My hand was on the door when he spoke.

"Bel?"

No one had called me that since my dad died. It shouldn't have sounded right coming from him, but it did. I hesitated, then looked back.

"Yes?"

"I thought I asked you to call me Kel?"

He slipped into the bathroom and quietly closed the door.

"Oh, boy." I fanned my hot face as I poured Addison his mega-serving of dog food, then brooded on the problem of Kelvin Kapone. He was a man who was obviously not any of those things on his business cards. I'd seen him get shot, spent the night with him, and I still didn't know who or what he was. Or what he thought about last night, about me. How much did he remember? What if he tried to kiss me again?

I discovered I was smiling and hastily straightened my mouth. It was obvious that thinking wasn't going to get me anywhere, so I opened the refrigerator and dug out some cold pizza, a tub of chocolate chip cookie dough and a liter of Pepsi. I paused, frowning.

Something was missing.

"Fruit. Of course." A former teacher ought to know her food groups better than that. I replaced the Pepsi with Cherry Coke, then cleared the cluttered top of my tiny breakfast bar, so I could set out paper plates, glasses and spoons. I finished my preparations just as Kel emerged from the bedroom.

He scrubbed up real good, even wearing slept-in, bled-upon pants. Nothing in his relaxed stance indicated injury except the white bandages across his mid-section.

He paused in the doorway and looked around. My apartment, which gave me an illusion of separation from my omnipresent family, covered the entire garage. The public part had been unevenly divided into a living room and kitchen, with most of the footage going to the living room. Since cooking wasn't high on my list of approved activities, I didn't mind.

Just past the kitchen was a hallway that led to the main house and the alcove where Addison habitually lurked in his crate when he wasn't hanging out with Rosemary's son.

My living room was mostly work area. The broken down couch and chair serving as spill over for my drafting table and desk. There were no shelves, the scummy Dag had fled with his bimbo before finishing that chore, so my books, sheet music, sketches, stereo, keyboard, and miscellaneous papers and magazines were stacked on furniture and floor.

Kel looked at me and I immediately went on the defense. "I know where everything is."

"I can see that." His intense gaze hooked mine, starting that weird stirring in my midsection. "That breakfast?"

"Uh, yeah—"

"Stan?" It was Rosemary in the hall outside my door and heading this way. "Are you up yet?"

"My sister!"

Kel and I looked at each other for a frozen moment. If I'd blinked, I'd have missed his panther-like retreat to my bedroom.

Rosemary poked her head around the door. Addison, now replete, almost knocked her over as he squeezed past her on his way to say good morning to Dominic.

Rosemary shut the door. "Are you all right? I thought I heard you fall or something?"

"I kind of fell out of bed."

Rosemary's brows arched. "Aren't you a little old to be falling out of bed?"

I arched mine back at her. "I didn't know there was an age limit."

She picked up a piece of pizza. "You haven't forgotten you're driving carpool this morning, have you?"

Carpool? Double dang. "No, I haven't forgotten. Why?"

"I thought maybe you'd like to meet me later, do some shopping? I want to pick up a girdle." She helped herself to a spoonful of cookie dough, leaving a dab of brown on her upper lip.

"Do they still make them?"

"Of course, only they call them body shapers." She took a bite of pizza, swallowed, then said, "Meet me one-ish?"

"Where?"

"Macy's?" When I nodded, she looked at her watch, dropped the half eaten slice back in the box and hopped off the stool. "Where're my car keys?"

The car. Oh, no.

"I left them in the car. It's in the garage."

I followed her out the door and down the stairs, although the last thing I wanted to do was be there when she hit the roof.

In the dim interior of the garage, the car looked dusty and innocuous, like cars in the winter when you can't keep them clean. The scrapes along the sides and roof, the bullet hole in the bumper seemed as bright as neon to me, but Rosemary didn't notice as she slid in. "I'll see you at one!"

It wasn't until she drove away that I remembered the gun that had fallen to the floor when Kel passed out. Had we done anything with it? Of course not. That would have been the sensible thing to do. Did it have a safety? Was it on or off? Off.

It had to be off. Kel had switched it off so he could shoot bad guys, but passed out.

Great, she'd be armed and dangerous. And I'd be the one she was hunting.

Kel was gone when I got back upstairs. I checked through the whole apartment just to be sure. In the bedroom the French doors were slightly open, the curtain still quivering as if from recent passage. I told myself I was glad and went back to the kitchen to clean up the uneaten breakfast. I only noticed the white square after I'd put the pizza away.

A business card.

I eyed it for a moment, wondering which profession he'd chosen. But it wasn't any of them. There wasn't a name, just a telephone and fax number and on the back in bold slashes: Thanks.

Chapter Six

"Ahoy, Captain." I peered cautiously into the bedroom of Rosemary's son, Dominic. I had good reason for caution. Dom thinks he's a pirate. As soon as he learned to count, he began counting the days until he could get a tattoo. Then he's heading to Florida so an alligator can bite his hand off. The plastic hook "hand" Rosemary bought him doesn't slash the way he'd like it to.

"Avast you scurvy dog!" he cried, turning to brandish his sword. He wore his "scalawag" gear, a red vest over his tee shirt, scabbard strapped over his jeans, eye patch, and a plumed tricorn hat.

"Ship sails in fifteen. Where's Addison?"

"Ar, Grandma made him go outside. He peed on her tree."

Why couldn't my dog learn to tell a silk tree from a fire hydrant? I decided to postpone greeting my mother. I left the scalawag in front of his preschool, feigned ignorance when he called the street monitor a desiccated bag of entrails, and went home to take Addison for his morning walk.

Addison and I have this system worked out, whereby he chooses where we go and I follow him. Then he will trot along beside me like I'm in charge. It works pretty well as long as no small, foreign cars drive by. He likes to eat their side mirrors.

Naturally he led me to the same park in which Kel and I had played "drive and shoot" last night. I let Addison off his leash and he took a moment to poke his head down a hole, before romping off to play with a couple of small children near the swings.

I stood with my hands shoved in the pockets of my soft, baggy jacket, the slight, chilly breeze ruffling the edges of my skirt, and looked around. The grass, brown and damp from last night's precipitation, still showed the crisscrossing tracks we'd made.

The pale, winter sunlight gave the whole park a forlorn air which exactly suited my merry-go-round thoughts about last night. Aimlessly I followed our tracks around the playground, my mind unrelentingly replaying each turn and jolt.

What was I going to do? I should go to the police, but what could I tell them that wouldn't get me locked up? I didn't have answers to the ethical or the practical questions and finally just put them aside. Which freed my brain to do a homing pigeon to what I really wanted to think about.

Kel. Would I see him again? Did I want to? Okay, I did, but did I dare see him again? I made it as far as the slab of cement, the smooth surface marred by two sets of tire tracks.

Addison bounded up and covered my face with huge, wet licks, almost knocking me over. I knelt down and buried my face in his smooth coat for a moment, letting the warmth of his body seep through to my chilled, scared center. When he wriggled to be free, I got up and clipped his leash back on. As we turned to leave, a familiar voice called my name.

I looked around and saw Flynn Kenyon waving at me as he walked across the grass. Sunlight achieved a moment of radiance by glinting off his soft white hair, cut expensively and brushed gently back from pale eyes capable of glowing hot. He was a tall, thin man with the patrician manner of the old-fashioned politico or salvation salesman. He sold business machines, which seemed a waste of his saintly aura.

When he wasn't selling typewriters, he was tirelessly devoted to community service. His statuesque, pedestal-like virtue might have made him insufferably stuffy if it weren't for his old world charm.

I liked him, though it seemed an impertinence.

"Good morning, Mr. Kenyon." I brushed at the grass clinging to my skirt, trying to bury my unease. Flynn used to be Rosemary's father-in-law and still is the grandfather of her children. I wasn't sure what that made him in my life.

"Why so formal? Just because Dag left his family, it doesn't mean I have." His voice was deep and rich, like New Orleans bread pudding drenched in rum sauce. His eyes twinkled slightly.

"Being called Isabel makes me feel formal."

"Ah, that explains Muir's singular lack of progress." The twinkle deepened. "He was disappointed not to see you last night."

"I was helping out with the youth choir."

"So he said." Addison sniffed his shoes and Flynn studied him thoughtfully. Addison returned the favor, only with his tongue hanging out. "So, this is The Dog."

Muir and Addison didn't like each other.

"He was walking me."

"Does he still bite off mirrors?"

I patted Addison's head. "Only foreign ones. He's very patriotic."

Flynn smiled kindly. I felt the lack of heavenly choir it called for and looked around for something to fill the silence instead. All I found was the cement slab. I rubbed it with my toe.

"What do you suppose this is for?"

"The pig."

"The pig?" Surely I hadn't heard him right.

Flynn smiled slightly. "An M114A2."

"A what?"

He grinned. It didn't suit him. His teeth weren't quite as perfect as the rest of him. "It's a howitzer. Artillery gun, towed."

"They're putting a howitzer in a park?"

"It's to be part of a memorial for the members of my Guard unit that died in foreign wars."

"Oh. Well, I'm sure it will be very . . . nice."

"The dedication ceremony is next Tuesday evening, part of a rally for our troops. Some of my former unit has already shipped out to the Gulf."

"Is this the God Bless the USA rally?"

He looked surprised. "Are you going to be there?"

"I play keyboard with Star Dust, you know, your back-up band for Lee Greenwood," I prompted.

"You play keyboard with young Jerome? Well, well. It ought to be an interesting evening, don't you think?" He smiled again, but this time the smile didn't reach his eyes. He stared into the distance as if he saw something besides a rally in a brown little park.

I stared, too. I was glad the howitzer hadn't been there last night.

I found Rosemary assessing long skinny tubes that looked like white Simpsons, but turned out to be the body shapers when I got to Macy's a bit after the agreed upon time.

"Sorry I'm late," I said, consciously casual. "I stopped to buy a new dress for my date."

"Since when do you buy clothes for Muir?"

I thumbed through a rack of mega bras. "Not Muir. Mike Lang."

Rosemary pulled me away from the bras. "Who?"

"Addison's vet."

"Really? Cute?" I nodded. She pulled a girdle off the rack. "We'd better get you shaped up for it, then."

I thought about Mike in his sigh-popping robe and nodded. "So how do we do this?"

"It all depends on what we want," Rosemary said. "If the problem area is the stomach, then we choose this one."

"What if it's everything?"

"We take this total control model that covers from boobs to knees."

I looked at the skinny tube doubtfully. "Does it come equipped with a safety valve? I don't want to end up in a Dave Barry column about exploding girdles because my cellulite breached containment."

Rosemary grinned. "With any luck it will push the flab up into the bra where we need it."

"It might do it for you," I said. "I'll probably just wind up with a fat neck and knees."

"Would you like to try that on?" a glacial voice asked behind me.

I jumped and found that what I'd thought was a mannequin was actually the sales clerk.

"She would," I said. Sometimes it was nice being identical. No need for both of us to squeeze into a three-inch tube in a hot, tiny dressing room.

I retreated to a sale table filled with filmy panties in neon colors. Everyone has to have a vice. Underwear was mine. I'd picked a handful when I heard the spine-tingling voice that I thought had passed from my life forever.

"There you are. Weren't you supposed to be here by one?"

I wanted to see him again, but not across a mound of neon panties. Sometimes it didn't pay to fall out of bed in the morning.

It didn't help that he looked more relaxed amid the lingerie than I did. I could see several women, including the mannequin sales clerk, giving him a twice over.

He did look fine, with no sign of injury visible to the naked eye. The color was back under his suntan and where his full length, navy coat fell open I could see soft gray pants elegantly hugging lean hips. His pristine white shirt, neatly buttoned and tie-wrapped, made him look clean, crisp, and very heroic.

Looking at him brought back all sorts of memories and feelings. My Sunday school teacher said we should hum hymns when faced with temptation.

Unfortunately, a "hallelujah" chorus, the only song that came to mind, did nothing to blunt temptation.

"What are you doing here?" I asked on a sigh.

"I need to talk to you."

"Oh?" Could he tell the heat turning my face into a beacon was for him? I peeked from under my lashes just in time to be on the receiving end of his hundred watt smile. The next thing I knew the panties I'd forgotten I was holding shot out of my hands as if launched by a slingshot. A purple pair landed on his shoulder. He snagged a scarlet pair out of the air.

His face carefully blank, he removed the purple, held it and the scarlet up. A careful and endless examination followed before he looked at me.

"Very nice. Do you want them?"

The ground refused to oblige me by opening at my feet. A disorderly retreat was clearly in order. "I . . . no, thanks."

I turned and crashed into a rack of bras. With diabolical swiftness Kel closed the distance and caught me against his chest. The rack was less fortunate. It went down with a crash, flinging bras everywhere. My heart gave an ecstatic leap, then settled into an unruly "Ode to Joy" because I was back where

I wanted to be. His heart thumped as wildly as mine, but I didn't know if it was for me or because he'd just leaped over a table full of panties into a storm of bras.

"You shouldn't . . . what about your . . ."

"I'm fine," he quickly cut me off.

He smelled good in an aggressively guy way. I inhaled him until my head spun, opened my eyes in a feeble effort to get my balance and saw us in a full length mirror. The bra caught in my hair was better than a cold shower.

The sales clerk minced up. Kel calmly set me back on my feet and began scooping up white mounds, tossing them onto the table with the neon panties.

I removed the bra, looked up and saw Kel watching me with humor, and something I was afraid to identify, sparking in his blue eyes.

I'd probably have stood there until I drooled, but the clerk said, coldly, "Were you going to buy that?"

I held it up. It was at least a 38D. "Yeah, right."

I handed it to her and walked away, chin up, spirit dragging. Kel caught up with me just as I was clearing the sexy nighties.

"Bel—"

"Please just go away." I would have been okay if I hadn't stopped and faced him. It put me at an immediate disadvantage because he was closer than I thought. His personal space wrapped around me like his arms had last night.

"It's important." He looked serious and sober.

"Look . . ."

"Stan?" Rosemary poked her head out of the dressing room and beckoned to me. I didn't see him fade away. He was just gone. My heart jumping, I stalked over to Rosemary.

"What?"

"Who's the guy?"

"Guy?" I couldn't explain Kel without revealing what I'd almost done to her car, so I had to play dumb.

"The guy you were talking to."

"I was talking to a guy?" I usually do dumb really well, but Rosemary's brows rose, her expression turned decidedly skeptical.

"You do know that men who hit on women in Lingerie are probably wearing it?"

"Of course." My gaze was bouncing around like a ping pong ball trying to spot him. I caught it and directed it her way. "I'm gonna go get something to drink."

"Bring me a Coke, would you?"

I nodded and found the escalator. I thought I was looking out for him, but he still managed to sneak up on me.

"Buy you a drink?" he whispered in my ear.

I jumped. My ear was delighted. My nerves less so. "I wish you'd quit doing that."

"Doing what?" He leaned against the side and grinned. He kind of reminded me, I decided, of a young Cary Grant. Not in looks, he was too yuppie and far too American. It was more an aura of reassuring rakishness and maybe something in the way he moved.

"Sneaking up on me." I tried to stay miffed, but it wasn't easy when he looked at me as if he liked what he saw.

"What did your sister say?"

I stepped off and turned to look at him, hands on my hips.

"That a man who hits on women in the Lingerie department is probably wearing it."

He chuckled. "Only one way I know for you to find out." He took my arm and steered me toward the food court. "Did she tell you I started to pick her up? You could be twins."

"We are twins."

"That would explain it." He stopped by a table under a red

and white striped umbrella, pulled out a chair and eased me into it. “Gave me quite a jolt when she turned around. Thought I was having a flashback from dog drugs.”

“You knew she wasn’t me?”

“Shouldn’t I have?”

I shrugged, obscurely pleased. “Most people have trouble telling us apart. Even her ex-husband claimed he couldn’t.”

“He was probably just trying to get a little on the side.” His eyes seemed to say, they understood why. “What’ll you have?”

I told him, he started to turn away, then stopped. “Wait here?”

It sounded like an order, but his gaze holding mine, made it a request I couldn’t refuse. I nodded. I had nothing to lose but my pride.

Chapter Seven

The table was barely big enough to hold two cold drinks and our knees rubbed together when Kel edged his chair in and rested his arm on the back of my chair.

Back in his personal space, I couldn't breathe or look away as his intense gaze drew me into a place that was both safe and terrifying. I vaguely remembered feeling like this the first time I saw Butch Cassidy and the Sundance Kid. The camera zoomed in for our first good look into Robert Redford's blue eyes and I turned into a puddle in the plush seat. To a lesser degree I also felt it the first time I saw Dudley Henderson, the star quarterback of my high school football team.

Neither of them had noticed me, but that hadn't stopped me from feeling so alive, I thought I'd die. I knew now people didn't die from a crush, but that didn't mitigate the dizzying sensation of rushing headlong into a terrifying unknown. It also didn't blunt the memory of how it felt when the object of my desire didn't return the longing. Just because Kel had been all over me last night, didn't mean he wanted *me*. He was drugged to the eyeballs, so last night couldn't be entered into evidence.

Today his gaze was a laser pinning me in place, but I still didn't know what to make of it. I opened my mouth, closed it, said, "What?"

If he hadn't been so close, I wouldn't have felt the start, or seen the edge of his mouth twitch briefly. He cleared his throat, but his voice still had a deeply husky edge when he said, “I need the purse.”

This was not what I’d expected him to say. “Purse?”

A hint of red crept under his smooth, tanned skin. “It’s a friend’s.”

“Right.” Like fizz from a soda bottle lust turned to giggles and rose in my throat.

He pushed a wispy bit of hair behind my ear. The brief touch, almost a caress helped me understand why cats purr when they are petted.

“I can’t explain why, but it’s critical I get that purse.”

The urgency underpinning his voice was a chilling reminder of how we’d come to meet. I opened my mouth to explain I didn’t have his purse—and realized I did. Or Rosemary did. “There was a purse in the car, maroon . . .”

“That’s it.” He leaned forward, his lean face tense. “Where is it?”

“It’s still under the seat—”

He stood up, bringing me with him. “Let’s go.”

So much for our drink.

“I have to get the keys from Rosemary—”

He had his arm around my waist, steering me toward the exit. Without missing a beat he shifted toward the escalator.

He had to let go when we got on, which did a lot to clear my thinking, though it didn’t take much brain power to conclude that the purse held some kind of a clue. I studied Kel surreptitiously. Was he an undercover cop? Or a private detective? If he was either of those things, he was going to be disappointed.

“You know, I looked through that purse last night. There wasn’t anything special in it.”

He helped me off the escalator, saying with a touch of condescension, “Sometimes things aren’t what they seem.”

Okay, if that's the way he wanted to play it, fine. Let him try to make a clue out of an adult diaper coupon. I opened my eyes really wide and said, "Oh?"

His gaze narrowed in on me. I held it for two long beats, then smiled. "I'll just get those keys for you."

I could feel him watch me walk away, but this time I didn't feel self-conscious. I felt good. I felt sassy.

I felt dangerous.

"Where did she say she parked?" Kel surveyed the parking lot like he could will Rosemary's Mercedes to step out of the pack. If cars had hearts, it would have worked.

"She said it was next to a purple van on this side of Macy's."

He looked at me. "A purple van?"

I shrugged. "It works for her."

"Bel—"

"Why do you call me that?" I looked down the row of cars instead of at him.

"Because Stan doesn't suit you and Isabel seems too formal—after last night."

Color burned into my cheeks. "Nothing happened last night." That was my story and I was sticking to it.

He chuckled and I had to look. The wind had whipped his hair into sexy disarray and put a glow in his face—just in case he wasn't potent enough to make a girl want to sing, "Baby, I'm yours."

"Not enough happened last night," he said.

My throat went dry in a heart beat. Heat from my cheeks spread like wildfire into other parts of my body. I needed a fire extinguisher. Or a tub of ice. "Does your wife know you flirt like this?"

His gaze narrowed. "I'm not married and you know it."

I arched my brows. "How would I know that? I don't know anything about you."

"Then why did you help me?"

I didn't have an answer. Luckily I spotted Rosemary's car. "There it is."

He turned and paced over to Rosemary's car. When he emerged from the car with purse and gun, he said, "My holster?"

I went blank for a minute. "Oh, Mike must still have it. I can get it from him tonight."

"Tonight? Don't worry about it."

Was that pique I heard in his voice? I hoped so. He shouldn't have it all his way. He shoved the gun in the back of his waistband, then looked at the purse awkwardly. I gave him a bland smile. He smiled sheepishly back.

"Don't want to be seen walking around with the evidence."

"Yeah, you might get asked out by a Congressman." How many times in my life had I used a quip to hide my heart from a man I wouldn't have minded sharing it with? I thought courage would come with maturity. Course, I thought maturity would come with age.

Kel grinned as he slammed the door and handed me the keys. "It wouldn't be the first time."

I smiled back. I couldn't help it. Something crackled across the distance. For an endless moment the sensation of contact arced the space that separated us. The world, the mall, the parking lot, all faded away, leaving me alone with him.

Several teenagers burst out the mall doors, breaking contact. Shouldn't they be in school? I wondered crossly.

Kel shifted slightly. "You have my card?"

I nodded.

"You can get hold of me if you think of anything or need anything. Just leave a message with the service."

"Sure—oh, I have a card, too." I rummaged through my purse, found the card case with a Junior Mint stuck to it, took one out, rubbed the cookie crumbs off on my jeans and handed it to him. "Marion made me put the little roach on it."

He took it, his lips twitching. "Very nice. You have a fax?"

"Yeah," I shrugged diffidently to hide the spurt of pride. I was the first in the family.

He grinned. "You'll have to—fax me sometime."

I had to smile. "I don't fax with just anyone."

"Not even—safe—fax?"

"Doesn't exist."

Was it regret I saw? He nodded, stepped back.

"Good-bye, Bel."

"Bye."

He disappeared among the cars with the swift grace of a big cat in dangerous territory.

If it had been a movie moment, the camera would have moved back, then higher until we were tiny separate specs in a sea of cars, mall and sky. The music, rising in crescendo, would be sad. It might even bring a tear to the eyes of anyone who'd ever watched a lover walk away in a swirl of memories and might-have-beens.

Only Kel wasn't my lover. There weren't a lot of memories on which to build my might-have-beens. I'd done the right thing, but it was cold comfort on a winter day when you're thirty-four and write children's books about a roach.

The wind cut through my coat and mental whine. I saw my hat and gloves in the back seat. I opened the car door and grabbed them. That's when I noticed a scrap of blue paper on the floor.

The typewriter repair claim ticket from the purse.

I must have dropped it last night. I frowned. It was hard to see what a broken typewriter could have to do with a suburban shoot out, particularly a typewriter in the tender care of the saintly Flynn Kenyon's company. But it was Kel's now. I'd have to get it to him.

I realized I was smiling and gave myself a shake. I needed to get a life, meet some men, kiss them or something. Oh, wait. I had a date with one tonight! Shouldn't be that hard to get him to kiss me.

I stuffed the slip in my coat pocket and smiled as I went to find Rosemary.

Chapter Eight

It was seven-fifteen when I finally turned my Honda into the driveway, the journey not made better by a news report about a shooting in the suburbs. It had to be Kel's shooting. There couldn't be two suburban shootings last night. What made it worse, I knew the victim, Elspeth Carter, from church. She was a good-hearted woman who volunteered a lot and couldn't help looking like Hitler. I felt awful and exhausted as guilt and my nearly sleepless night caught up with me.

Three hundred and sixty-four days in a year I would have loved a date with a guy like Mike. He had to ask me out on the one day I'd rather be premenstrual.

This is one of the reasons why I have never married.

I passed through the kitchen to let my mother know I wouldn't be eating supper, got chewed out for sneaking a chocolate chip cookie, then grilled about my date with Mike.

"A dog doctor. Couldn't he get into a real medical school?"

"He's an over achiever. He wanted something harder than a real medical school." I made a show of looking at my watch and exclaimed in horror. "He's picking me up at eight and I don't want to be late."

She let me pass, but followed me down the hall.

"You known him long?"

"Just since I got Addison."

Now she was following me up the stairs.

"Does he live alone?"

"As far as I know."

We were heading down the hall. I could see my door.

"Maybe he'd like a home-cooked meal? I'll bet he eats out a lot. You and your young man could eat with us?"

My young man. If only she knew how true that was. Mike had to be at least five years younger than me. I opened my door and turned to face her.

"I don't think so."

"You could ask him, Isabel."

"We've already got reservations at his favorite restaurant."

"Oh?" She didn't say it, but the question was there, hanging in the air between us. I tried to fight it, but I've been giving in to the woman for thirty-four years.

"It's this quaint little place called," my mind raced, but instead of quaint it produced, "The Tandoor Club."

I groaned inside as the name from the matchbook slipped out. Maybe Mike liked Moroccan food. And if he didn't, perhaps the exotic dancers would distract him.

On the outside the Tandoor Club looked plain and uninteresting. Inside it was a bona fide Arabian Nights. A silk-draped opening held back with gold tassels gave the illusion of entering a tent. A huge mock brazier gave the impression of a fire while music filtered out of a snake charmer's flute at the center of the room. Persian rugs were spread beneath low tables surrounded by heaped pillows and lounging bodies that struck a wrong note with their Western clothing. Dancing girls weren't dropping grapes into mouths, but turbaned waiters glided around the room holding large trays of exotic looking food.

I was used to strange scents. I'd lived in New Orleans. But

this was like nothing I'd ever smelled. The tangle of incense, tobacco smoke and rich spices carried hints of magic and mystery, stirring my latent sleuth instincts like a mischievous finger.

What if the matchbook was The Clue? It certainly made more sense than the adult diaper coupon.

As Mike and I settled on our pillows, I scanned the murky interior for suspects. Next to me Mike shifted cushions, trying to find a comfortable position on the pillows.

"Are you okay?"

Due to the ruthless combination of body shaper and little black dress, he was able to leer good-naturedly at my generously exposed legs. "No. But the view helps."

I tugged at the hem, which unaccountably slipped higher.

"Don't be stingy," he advised. "You have great legs."

"Really?" I surveyed them doubtfully.

"It's one of the first things I noticed after you pulled your dog off me that day."

Well, what's a girl to do after a nice compliment like that? Particularly in light of my new determination to get kissed? I smiled and let my hem wander where it wanted. Never let it be said that I was stingy with my legs.

Mike settled into the cushions and surveyed our surroundings with something like awe. "So, this is your favorite restaurant?"

"Actually, this is your favorite restaurant." He looked surprised, so I added, "My mother."

He'd met my mother when he picked me up and didn't need further explanation. He grinned. "I have interesting taste."

Since he was sitting here with me, because of me, I had to agree. We did the polite chit-chat see-saw, this took us through ordering, then the floor show started, effectively ending chit, chat, and Mike's focus on me.

I have this theory that there was only so much available bosom to be divided among the women of the world. Since I didn't get my share, I've often wondered who did. The floor show answered that question.

Akasma, the climbing flower of Casablanca got mine.

Plus that of a few dozen other girls.

These were not mere boobs attached to her chest. She had breasts. Gazooms. Hooters. Jugs—and every other nickname a man has given the female bosom. Akasma had the Tetons of Tetons, twin peaks of magnificence, that bobbed and undulated insistently as she performed the ancient dance of her forebears with a sinuous grace and even more amazing flexibility.

She could have beat herself to death with her own flesh, but the only casualty was my ego. What were a pair of great legs compared to white hills cut by plunging valley a guy could dive down in to his ankles? Mike didn't just stare with a round "O" of amazement at the center of his black beard. He drooled.

Him and every other man in the room.

It had seemed cool, almost cold when we arrived. Not anymore. By the time Akasma was halfway through her show, you could have fried bread. To a crisp.

If that weren't bad enough, my "flexible and comfortable" body shaper decided it was time to contract to its original ten by three inch, pre-donning configuration. My lungs felt like they were being squeezed up out my nose. Everything else felt like it was getting squeezed out the bottom. I needed air. If I passed out right now, no one would notice.

"Got to powder my nose, Mike," I croaked. With my elegant three inch heels, it wasn't easy to get my feet under me. Through the red haze forming in front of my eyes, my thighs were turning into pencils and my knees into mini-blimps as my shaper continued its drive toward my spine. I figured I'd reach critical mass in about five. At which point, my head and my feet would pop off. The fact that I'd be left with a body a model would envy was small comfort.

"You couldn't fake that, could you?" Mike asked in awe, oblivious to my inelegant rise from the pillows. Why should he look at me when he had one of the great wonders of the world undulating in his face?

"I've never been able to," I squeezed out before tottering in the direction of the Ladies. My tongue hung out, no room in my mouth anymore. I barely made it in the door, started clawing at inflexible elastic before the door swung shut. With the distant wail of Akasma's music filtering in, I shimmied out of the shaper and threw it across the room, then leaned on the sink and drew in great, gulping breaths of bathroom scented air and was grateful for it.

I wanted to go home. My battle with the shaper had drained what little enthusiasm I had left. Mike wouldn't notice me as long as Akasma was shaking her booty, I thought sourly.

I left the bathroom, brooding on fate's cruelty. About halfway along the hallway, as I was passing a narrow side passage, a strong arm hooked around my waist, a hand covered my mouth, and without ceremony I was half dragged, half lifted backwards into the recess.

"Bel?" A familiar voice spoke in my ear.

Kelvin Kapone. Why was I not surprised? For the second time that night I sagged in relief.

"You have got to stop doing that," I said, severely, turning in his arms to face him. "You've already taken twenty years off my life expectancy. At this rate, I'm gonna die last week!"

"Sorry." He flashed his grin. I tried to steel my heart

against it. A grin should only be able to take you so far, no matter how endearing. "I wanted to talk to you on the QT."

"Really?" I arched my brows and stepped back to look him over. He was wearing one of the waiter's turbans and a flowing burnoose. He looked great. "Have you considered the telephone? Marvelous invention for anonymous communication . . ."

"Bel." He put a finger lightly across my smart mouth, immediately reducing it to stupid. "This is serious. What are you doing here?"

Being humiliated. "Having supper. What are you doing here dressed like Ali Baba?"

Not that I was complaining. White was definitely his color, deepening his blue eyes and showcasing his tan.

"Doing a little unofficial snooping. Isn't that why you're here? Because of the message in the matchbook?"

"What message in what matchbook?"

"The one in the purse. You said you looked through it." He leaned against the wall with his arms crossed, his eyes slightly narrowed as he waited for my response.

"I was looking for ID, not clues." Something nudged at the edge of my mind, something about the purse. "I'm not exactly the sleuthing type."

"Good. Keep it that way."

That made me bristle. "Why is it okay for you to sleuth and not me? Are you some kind of cop?"

"I'm not any kind of cop."

"Right." This time I crossed my arms and leaned against the wall. "And your gun?"

"Don't ask questions, Bel, unless you're sure you'll like the answers."

I stared at him for a moment as a chill made its way down my back. "That almost sounded like a threat."

"It's a friendly warning." He leaned in, his hands resting on the wall on either side of my head. "So you won't get hurt. Whoever was shooting last night, got a good look at me. I'm probably not the safest person for you to be seen with."

"Oh." The pre-Akasma chill returned in spades. Once more, I saw the round-headed guy framed in the open window. Had he seen me? I shuddered, felt the goose bumps pop out on my arms. I wasn't kidding when I said I wasn't the sleuthing type. "Then maybe I should get back to Mike."

"Ah yes, the doc." He straightened and crossed his arms. He almost sounded miffed. "You know, he's not your type."

Warm pushed at the chill as the balance of power shifted back my way. "You haven't even known me for twenty-four hours and you know what my type is?"

His smile had a bit of wolf to it. "But it's been such a busy day, it seems longer."

I couldn't argue with that. Just moments ago I'd been wondering if it would ever end. Now I was wondering about the ethics of wanting to kiss one guy, while on a date with another. Maybe it was because Mike was still an unknown while I knew what kissing Kel was like.

Kel was close, but not close enough. The air in the small space was super-charged and I knew in my quivering gut he was feeling what I was. Maybe not for the same reasons; men were aliens after all. Perhaps he was only interested in good fax. The power of being desired, in a strange way, gave me the resolution I needed to deny us what we both wanted.

"I have to go."

"Yes." He took one step back. "No more sleuthing?"

I smiled slightly, feeling old and wise, and shook my head.

He stood there, looking like the gorgeous sheik of something.

"Take care, Bel."

"I will. You take care, too. Watch that wound." I smiled feebly. "I'm fresh out of underwear."

His gaze was scorching as it swept up, then down my body. "I can see that. Anyone ever tell you that you have magnificent legs?"

This time my smile wasn't feeble. Magnificent was better than great. Kind of took the sting out of Akasma.

"Maybe."

I knew he watched me walk away, and I knew the moment he quit watching. I felt part of me leave with him. I hoped it wasn't my heart. I only had the one.

Chapter Nine

I got back just as Mike tucked some money into Akasma's wispy pants, but I was in no position to call him on it.

We ate silently, Mike's thoughts presumably on amazing breasts, mine fixed on Kel and the mystery. I wasn't born to sleuth, but I did have the normal amount of curiosity. A promise to not sleuth didn't preclude wondering. Why was Kel here disguised as a waiter? What message had he found? My pastry stuffed chicken turned to ashes in my mouth as another thought pattered through my brain. What if the round-headed man showed up here?

I did another surreptitious survey, but there were no round heads in my vicinity. I turned my musings back in Kel's direction. It was kinder to my digestion. Not a cop, he said. Could he be a private detective? I examined the idea from all sides and decided I liked it. Pleased with this minor, though unconfirmed, bit of deduction I studied the crowd again. My problem was, I wouldn't have recognized a clue if it came up and spoke to me.

"Rosemary?"

Not a clue. A jerk. I looked up with extreme reluctance.

My sister's scum bag ex, was looking down at my legs. Where Flynn Kenyon was light, Dag Kenyon was shadow. Dark hair, dark eyes, dark soul and bimbo-deep in the second year of his mid-life crisis.

Muir didn't look like either of them, though I couldn't remember precisely how, despite our long, tepid association. He was the ultimate, out-of-sight, out-of-mind, forgettable guy.

I gave Dag a frigid look that bounced off his ego. "Still trying to pretend you can't tell us apart? Isn't it a bit redundant now that Rosemary doesn't want you either?"

"Isabel." His smile was thin and cold, his eyes a dead zone. He looked at Mike and his oddly light brows arched in a question I had no intention of answering.

I didn't care if I was Baptist. I wasn't about to forgive him for what he did to my sister.

"I could have sworn Muir said he had a date with you tonight?"

"Really?"

"I had no idea you were involved with someone else." He looked at Mike again.

"I can't think of any reason why you should know." Mike's voice was quiet, but there was a hint of menace darkening his eyes. I knew his massive shoulders weren't just for show and hoped Dag provoked him into flexing them.

Dag looked at the shoulders and chose discretion. "I'm Dag Kenyon, Isabel's brother-in-law—"

"Ex-brother-in-law."

Mike rose from the cushions, his bulk casting a shadow over Dag. "Mike Lang, Isabel's vet."

"Really? And how is your huge hound, Isabel?"

I felt a chill. Surely he hadn't seen Rosemary's car parked outside Mike's house last night?

"He still doesn't like you."

"Can't win them all." He stepped back, flicking us both another mocking glance. "It was so charming to see you again. I won't give Muir your love." He turned away, but before I could sigh with relief, he paused to deliver one last salvo, "Oh, Dad was right." He let the pause lengthen painfully, before adding, "You do look intriguing today. What have you been up to?"

Before I could answer, he gave me a mocking salute, then turned and slithered back into the shadows from whence he came.

"Nice guy," Mike said, resuming his pillows.

I sank down. "A real gem. Rosemary and I usually fall for the same guys, but he was the exception. I don't know what she saw in him that I didn't."

"Maybe that you didn't like it was the attraction?" Mike said. "Couldn't have been easy to always look like someone else."

Talk about illuminating the obvious. I couldn't believe I hadn't seen it before. And of course, I'd resisted marriage and moved to New Orleans to prove I didn't care. Poor Rosemary sure paid a heavy price for autonomy, I decided sadly, watching Dag pay his tab and then usher his bimbo of the moment out the door. He looked back long enough to give me a mocking salute. I barely resisted the urge to give him a one-finger salute in return.

"Do you think he saw the car outside your house last night?" I asked.

"It isn't the only Mercedes around."

"He has a particular interest in this car." And what if he saw more than just the car?

"Does it matter?"

"Probably not." I tried to shrug away the uneasy feeling that it did matter while we finished our dessert. I was glad to leave the stuffy den for the cold outside, even more glad for Mike's big body providing some shelter from the breeze whipping across the parking lot. His arm over my shoulders was comforting, but it didn't weaken a single bone in my body as we strolled in the direction of his car.

Dozy and stuffed with good food, my gaze passed right over the round silhouette without it registering on my internal Richter scale for several steps.

I stopped, looked back and saw nothing.

"Stan?" Mike pulled gently on my arm.

Further down the line of cars, I sensed, rather than saw movement. Without thinking I pulled away from Mike and took a few steps in that direction.

"My car's this way . . ."

"Did you see someone over there?" I didn't consider this sleuthing. It was being careful. "There, did you see that?"

"So, there's someone there. What of it? This is a parking lot." Mike sounded understandably bewildered.

I saw a minivan pull away from a line of cars and turn toward the street. In just a moment it would have to pass under the street light.

I pressed forward, caught my heel on something on the ground and went sprawling. The landing was surprisingly soft.

What—

In my peripheral vision I saw an ear. Before I could stop myself, I turned and looked. A face. A face with a thin line of something dark oozing down from the hole in his temple . . .

My jaw dropped.

I sipped the coffee Mike had brought me and leaned against a police car, the flashing blue lights tracing a constant path across my feet, heightening the feeling that I'd wandered onto a crime drama cop show. All around me official types were stringing tape, taking pictures and asking questions. No one was drawing chalk outlines, which I found vaguely disappointing. I decided I was in shock. With detached calm, I spotted Mike making his way through the throng of police people. He looked so normal, so real, it was almost obscene.

"How are you feeling?"

I managed a wan smile. "I'm fine. I'm sorry I lost it. I had no idea I was a screamer."

"It's a nasty business."

"Do they—" I had to swallow twice before I could get past the clump of fear clogging my throat. "—know who it was?"

"It's a kid." He shook his head. "I heard someone mention drugs."

Someone had died. Someone's son or brother. I wanted to cry, but I was too tired. And so very cold, my tears would probably be ice cubes. I couldn't seem to stop shuddering. They'd start as small, little quivers across the surface of my skin, raising goose bumps on their way, then grow into these great, quaking shudders that made my bones ache and rattled my teeth.

"I want to go home." I looked up at him with a pitiful look that wasn't faked.

While Mike went to check, I stood up and tried out my legs with some pacing. My teeth didn't chatter so bad when I kept moving. I wasn't surprised when Kel pulled me into the shadow of 4x4 pickup truck. It seemed inevitable.

"What happened?" he asked.

"Happened?" Although I could hardly see him, he'd lost the burnoose for a clothes black-out, I looked away. "What happened? I tripped on a body. That's what happened!"

"How did you manage that?"

There was a hint of amusement in his voice that brought my hackles up. It wasn't his fault, I knew it in my mind, but in my heart I felt like it was all his fault. I'd managed to get through four years in New Orleans without involvement in any kind of crime. Less than twenty-four hours after meeting him, I was involved in two murders. Coincidence?

Maybe. If you believed in fairy tales.

"I thought I saw the round-headed man."

"The . . . who?"

"The round-headed man. From last night. You know, in the green minivan that chased us? The guy who killed Mrs. Carter. I thought—aren't you here looking for him?"

"I didn't see the man who shot at me." He stepped close, enveloping me in the spicy scent of his after shave, mixed liberally with cooking smells from the Tandoor Club. It was pretty yummy, even on a full stomach and in shock to my eyeballs. "You saw the man who shot at us? Why didn't you tell me?"

"You didn't ask."

There was a short silence. "Did he see you?"

"Tonight? I don't think so."

"No, last night. Did he see you last night, when you saw him? Does he know you saw him?"

"I don't know." Yummy faded abruptly. People who can identify killers get killed. This was not good. "I wish Mrs. MacPhearson hadn't got the flu!"

Kel looked at me, opened his mouth, closed it, and shook his head. "Are you sure it was the same man?"

"Of course not. I only saw his silhouette. But he drove off in a minivan—and no, I don't know if it was the same one. In case you hadn't noticed, it's dark out."

I was rapidly descending into grumpy. I was tired and I wanted to go home. And worst of all, I wanted my mother. I'd been reduced to that. "Are you, like, a private detective or something?"

He went tense. "Why do you ask?"

Had I struck a nerve? "John Q. Citizen you're not. I'm not stupid, you know."

Okay, so maybe he didn't know, but he could give me the benefit of the doubt. I challenge anyone to shine after getting shot at and tripping over a body.

"I never thought you were." He hesitated, then said, lightly, "Not a bad bit of deduction." I felt an inappropriate thrill of pleasure until he added, "I thought we agreed you wouldn't sleuth?"

I drew myself up haughtily. "I wasn't sleuthing. I was thinking. There is a difference." A fine one, but still a difference.

He smiled, the white of his teeth cutting the darkness—and my angst—in half. "I guess I can't fault you for thinking. I've been thinking, too." He hesitated. "About you."

"Really?" Yummy was making a comeback, but I was still suspicious. "What about me?"

He hunched his shoulders, the action shifting him slightly into what little light there was. Or maybe my eyes were just adjusting. I could see his eyes, the blue shining like a beacon in the dark, but the expression in them was less clear. I had a feeling he was uncomfortable—or nervous.

"I've just . . . never met anyone like you."

I was trying to decide if this was a compliment or not, when I heard someone call my name. I turned in the direction of the voice—and felt the brush of cool air carrying Kel's scent as he slipped away like a will-o'-the-wisp. If he didn't stop doing that . . .

"Miss Stanley?" The man flashed his badge, his voice abrupt, but not unkind. "I'm Detective Dillon of the Homicide Division. I'd like to ask you a few more questions before you leave, if you don't mind."

"Couldn't this wait?" Mike spoke behind him. "She's already given two statements to two officers already."

"It's okay, Mike. He probably needs further clarification on a few points." I gave the detective a helpful look.

"You have that down mighty pat, Miss Stanley," Dillon said, suspiciously instead of gratefully.

"I'm a Columbo fan."

"Wonderful." The detective flipped open a notebook.

"I'm glad you're feeling better, Stan," Mike said, dryly.

"So am I." I sighed a little. He was such a nice guy and Kel was right, Mike wasn't my type.

"Then you won't mind answering a few questions?"

"No, detective, I don't mind. Though I don't know what else I can tell you." Actually there was a lot I could have told him. But none of it concerned this particular murder.

"According to your statement," the detective said, "you don't know the victim?"

"No." I studied the detective curiously, wondering why he looked familiar to me. He was a handsome man, about my height, with big dark eyes and a strong chin. "Have we met somewhere before?"

"I don't think so," he said, impatiently. "Does the name Paul Mitchell mean anything to you?"

"Hair care." Both men looked blank. "Awaphui Shampoo. Hair conditioner. The ultimate cure for split ends."

Mike grinned. The detective looked annoyed.

"Paul Mitchell is the victim's name."

"Oh. I'm sorry. I didn't know."

"Dr. Lang indicated that his car is parked several lanes over that way. Why did you walk down the lane where the body was, Miss Stanley?"

This was a tricky part. I plastered on what I hoped was an innocent look and offered a half truth. "I thought I saw someone I recognized."

"In a dark parking lot?"

"It was a nagging impression of familiarity. You know how it is."

His face said he didn't. His eyes narrowed for the kill. "And were you right? Was it someone you knew?"

I didn't flinch. "I don't know. I tripped and fell before I found out."

He shook his head, hunching his shoulders impatiently. I knew I'd seen that movement before.

"Are you sure we haven't met? What did you say your name was?"

"Dillon. Now look, Miss Stanley . . ."

"You're not related to Drumstick Dillon, are you?"

"You know my son?" That got his attention.

"I knew you looked familiar. You're two peas in the same pod."

He looked at me thoughtfully. "You have a good eye, Miss Stanley."

"Stan is an illustrator," Mike told him.

It sounded better than, she draws cartoon roaches.

"I see," Dillon said, his gaze intent enough to make me uneasy. "How do you know my son?"

"I play keyboard in his band."

"His band." His brows shot toward his ruthlessly subdued Afro. "How . . . unusual."

"Me?" I shook my head emphatically. "I'm not unusual. Actually I'm the most ordinary person I know. Boring. Dull."

Dillon and Mike regarded me with unrelenting and obvious skepticism. Mike I could understand, but what was Dillon's problem? I smiled uneasily.

"Really. Boring."

"Let's go over your statement again," Dillon said.

Chapter Ten

Dillon finally let me go home, though I could tell he still wasn't satisfied with my story. The guy had good instincts. I'll bet his son didn't get away with a thing.

Mike accompanied me inside and met Rosemary. I saw attraction sparks arc between them and form a weld, but was too tired to care that Rosemary was going to get my good-night kiss.

My mother had already retired to her bed, so I didn't have to explain how it was I'd come to trip over a dead body outside a sleazy restaurant. In my dreams, I tripped over bodies and got shot at all night. When I stumbled down the stairs the next morning, feeling like old road kill, I found Rosemary preparing to go out wearing designer jeans and a bulky sweater, with guilt as an accessory.

Careful not to make eye contact she asked, "Tell Mom I'm breakfasting out, okay?"

"Sure." I let her get her hand on the door before adding, "Tell Mike I said hi."

She gave me an apprehensive look. "How did you know?"

"I have a gift for seeing the obvious." She looked so worried I had to relent. "Have fun."

Rosemary's smiled was relieved. "Really?"

"Really." I shrugged. "He's not my type anyway." And it would make a good forgiveness card to play when she found out about her car. She left and Candice came in. She was wearing jeans and a big sweater that looked like it came out of her mother's closet. I looked closer. It came out of my closet. "Nice sweater, Candy."

"Thanks." She didn't even blink. "So, how was your date?"

"Fine, until I tripped over the dead body."

"Cool." She opened the refrigerator and took a pudding. "Tell Gram I don't have time for breakfast, okay?"

"You can tell me yourself, Candice." We both spun guiltily to face her. "I may be old, but I'm not hard of hearing."

"Sorry, Gram. Got a study hall before school." She made the detention sound so normal, I smiled. Not that I was about to rat on her. If she wasn't setting off my mother's highly honed guilt sensors, more power to her.

"We're hungry, Gram," a chorus chimed. Rosemary's twins, matching owls also in jeans and sweaters popped out from behind my mother. I could see a theme developing here. Only my mother was refusing to fall in the party line. She was wearing her customary casually dressy pants suit. Not a cozy grandma, but definitely a fond one. Her whole face lit up. When she'd determined what their breakfast desire was, she turned to me.

"How are you feeling today, Isabel?" The question was asked with unusual delicacy. Someone must have told her about the body.

"I'm fine." I didn't shuffle my feet, but only because I had on rubber-soled shoes.

"Good." She looked like she wanted to say more. I was relieved when she turned and began assembling pancake ingredients, until she asked, "Where's your sister?"

"Rosemary?"

"Do you have another sister?"

I laughed weakly. "She's out."

I got a patient look. "Where?"

"She's got a date," Joelle, the diminutive traitor informed her. Kids. Why do people have them?

Mother looked at me, brows at full arch. "A date? With whom?"

The million dollar question. Rosemary was out with my vet and I was going to get in trouble for it. Life was so unfair.

"With Mike Lang."

"Your Mike Lang?"

"He's not my Mike Lang. He's my vet. And a friend."

"A friend. That's what you always say. You couldn't try to be attracted to one of these friends?"

I could have told her how attracted I could be. I could have told her about Kel. About kisses that made me sizzle like a Roman candle and turn as squishy as warm butter. I could have told her I was so attracted to him, I darn near jumped his bones the first night I met him.

I could have, but I'm not stupid. My mother wanted me to be attracted, not hot to trot. I just shrugged and looked clueless. I was good at it, because I usually am.

My mother sighed, blowing guilt through clueless, like it was a sieve. "Muir called for you last night. He seemed to think you had an arrangement to discuss his computer program."

"Really? When people want an arrangement with someone, they should ask, not just assume. All he said was that he'd call."

"Well, he did call. And so did Reverend Hilliard." My mother looked happier thinking about the good Reverend.

Which increased my unhappy level. "What did he want?"

"He wanted to know if you'd play the organ for Elspeth

Carter's funeral on Saturday. I told him that you would be delighted."

"Should I be delighted to play for a funeral?"

"You should always be delighted to help out."

The Gospel according to Mother. She interpreted it with the same ruthlessness as Henry the Eighth. I could almost feel the marital ax inch closer to my neck. The telephone rang under my elbow. I jumped for it and knocked the receiver to the floor. I had to reel it in before I could say hello.

"Stan? Glad I caught you. Marion here." Marion was my editor. I liked her, even though she made me keep producing roach books for a strangely adoring bunch of weird kids and was younger than me. I had to face it, about half the world was younger than me now.

"How are you? You sound close, like you're right here in town."

"I am right here in town. I came for the convention."

"Oh. How nice." Convention? Her voice told me I should know what she was talking about so my mind tried to race, but it was kind of out of shape after my double crime whammy.

"I knew you'd forget about tomorrow."

"Tomorrow?" A vague memory tried to surface.

"The IRA convention. Autographs at ten?" she reminded me with a hint of steel in her voice.

"Oh, that," I said with a large round of indifference. "How could I forget that?"

"I knew you'd try."

"Well, so would you if you had to sign your name to a bug's butt. Don't the people who buy my books scare you?"

"No, you scare me when you try to write those lame romances. Please tell me you've given it up?"

"I have." My tone didn't convince me either.

"You're not a romantic."

"I can be romantic!" My mother and Marion snorted at the same time. I snapped, "Fine. Just tell me where to be tomorrow. I'll happily devastate my carpal tunnels for your filthy lucre."

"Thank you." She gave me directions and rang off.

"I told Muir you'd call him back," my mother said.

"And I will. Later. After I get back from my rehearsal."

My mother snorted again, but I told myself she was just blowing her nose. It could be that. Cold air made everyone's nose run.

When I rang the bell at Jerome's house, his father answered the door. Steven Jeffries, Major, retired, was an older version of his son. Erect and lean, his salt and pepper hair was still cut military style. It was immediately obvious he was suffering from a serious case of war-watching syndrome.

We spent a few minutes discussing smart bombs and the options for ground war, while I wondered how a military establishment that paid two hundred dollars for a toilet seat had managed to create a bomb with intelligence. When he paused for air, I asked for Jerome.

"He's out back in the garage." He hesitated, looking at me with an intensity that made me wonder what I'd done. "There's something different about you today, Miss Stanley."

"Different?" Pinned in his gaze, I felt just like I did in the dream where I'd forgotten my pants and didn't know it until I was in a wide, open space with a lot of other people. I did a surreptitious check to make sure I had on everything I was supposed to.

"Why don't," he went to an "at ease" posture and gave me a frightening smile that I suspect he meant to be friendly. It didn't go with the crew cut and the posture. "—you call me Steve?"

Steve? I almost croaked with fright when he stepped closer. I stepped back.

"I don't think—"

I might as well have not spoken. We were practically doing the Tango around the room.

"Jerome calls you Stan, I know, but that's not the name for a beautiful woman."

"That's why they call me Stan," I pointed out feebly. Miss America I'm not.

"Isn't your name Isabel?"

"Well, yes, but all my friends call me Stan." I saw the door off to my right and started edging that way.

"Would you consider having dinner with me some night, Isabel." Somehow he got hold of my hand.

I cleared the squeak out of my throat and said, like I'd never heard of it, "Dinner?"

He smiled complacently. "A meal taken in the evening."

He actually thought I was suffering from maidenly confusion, not a stupor of thought brought on by horror. I opened my mouth to say no, not ever, but out popped, "Well, okay, I guess I could think about it."

My lack of enthusiasm brought on more of his frightening approval. He probably thought maidenly confusion had given way to maidenly modesty.

"Saturday night? We could take in the bingo tournament and dance a few polkas after. They have a gal that plays a brisk accordion."

I felt for the knob behind me as panic put a choke hold on my throat. Bingo? Brisk accordion polkas? Was God punishing me for my near romp with Kel? If He was, He'd chosen the perfect vehicle for it.

I choked, which he took for assent.

"Pick you up at four? You aren't one of those modern gals who can't eat until midnight, are you?"

I shook my head. If I were, I wouldn't have a date with a man old enough to be my father. I made this gesture toward the garage where Jerome waited.

Steve stepped back. "No need to mention this to the boy."

The boy. I almost moaned. I shook my head again.

In the garage, "the boy" looked up from his guitar.

"Yo, Stanley! What's happening?"

I tried not to look hunted. "Nothing. Nothing at all." I could feel a confession coming on and looked around in panic. "Where's everybody? I thought I was late. Not that I was doing anything to make me late, you understand."

"They'll be along. I had a little business to discuss with you so they cleared off." He folded up one leg, looking vaguely Jimmy Dean-ish and studied me, a look in his eyes that suddenly reminded me of his father.

Was guilt written large on my face? I had so much to feel guilty about, it had to be written in neon. I turned away. What could I say to him? I took a deep breath and turned to face him. "Jerome . . ."

He tipped his head to one side. "You look different."

What was it with everyone? Flynn. Dag. Steve. And now Jerome. I wasn't different. They were.

He patted the crate next to him with a smile that, unlike his dad's, really was inviting. "Park it and let's shoot the breeze for a mo."

Experience had taught me this was an invitation to sit down, so I took the indicated spot. "Okay. Shoot."

"The thing is, we all think you're fine."

"Thank you." I think. Had I missed something somewhere?

"You're welcome. And we, the three of us, were wondering if you'd, like, like to go out with us?" he finished in a rush, then sat back relieved.

I'd definitely missed something somewhere. "I go out with you all the time."

"For gigs."

"Which are out," I pointed out.

"Like we were wondering if you'd make it personal, or was it, like, against your code to mix extreme pleasure with business?"

Either Jerome was more like his dad than either of us suspected or I was suffering from the onset of menopause. I felt like I'd been going up hill and discovered it was actually down hill. "You want?"

"A date. We all do."

First the father, now the son? Something was seriously wrong here.

"With me?" I had to be sure.

"With you." Jerome grinned, but there was a tenseness about him that was, well, sweet. Still . . .

"Will there be cameras involved?"

"No cameras," the grin widened into a smile loaded with youthful charm. "Like I said, you're fine." He stood up, shoved his hands into the pocket of his tight jeans and paced away. Then he paced back towards me. Did I mention the jeans were really tight? Or that he had a great, practically world class butt?

What was my problem? Just yesterday I'd identified a need to kiss men. Now here were men, or at least men in the making, willing to oblige me. Well, willing to take me out in public.

"What did you have in mind?"

"Everything of the most sensitive, I promise. We've

been reading Cosmopolitan."

That gave me pause. "Really."

"We were thinking a club, like The Rad?"

"I've never been there," I admitted.

"It's fine. Thought we'd all go, like together, no pressure, and then after you can decide."

"Decide?"

"Who you want to take you home. You know, the good-night kiss. Can't all huddle on your doorstep. Seriously not sensitive." He looked cheerful and strangely business-like. Jerome was going to go far. "So, what do you say?"

He lacked the wattage of Kel, but made up for it with youthful enthusiasm. And he was willing to commit to kissing before the date. Just because I'd be both the younger and older woman to relatives was no reason to pass up a great opportunity to replace Kel in my head.

"If you're sure—"

"Truly fine!" He looked seriously delighted. It was a strange sensation, knowing I'd caused it. Then Tommy and Drum appeared in the doorway and indulged in some high fives and back slapping when they were told about my positive response to their experiment. It was very flattering. Maybe I ought to almost get killed more often.

"Can we pick you up around ten thirty? Don't want to get there too early. Just soon enough to get a table. It's, like, a happening place."

"Ten-thirty's not too early for you, is it?" Drum asked anxiously. What a contrast with his suspicious father.

I looked at their tight, young bodies, and fresh eager faces. They have two-thirds of their lives ahead of them, but I probably only had half left. Was it fair to feed my ego with their youth and enthusiasm? It gave me a serious qualm, but I was able to quell it.

They might be young, but they were resilient. If it didn't work out, they'd get over it quicker than I would. While we set up for the practice, I did a mental scan of my planner. Convention tomorrow, date with three young men Friday night, a date with the father of young man Saturday afternoon, and funeral in between. No problem.

Chapter Eleven

With the guys' sensitivity well established and the details of our date worked out, we then got down to practicing. It was a good thing I waited until we were done before I mentioned I'd tripped over a body last night. They clustered around me like cute ghouls until I mentioned that victim's name was Paul Mitchell.

There was a short silence.

"Couldn't be our Paul Mitchell," Tommy said, without conviction. "He's not the kind of guy to get snuffed. Too straight arrow."

Jerome sounded equally unconvinced. "He's Guard. Shipping out for the Gulf next week, right after the rally."

But we all knew it *was* their Paul.

As Jerome so elegantly put it, major bummer of a day. At least it couldn't get any worse. Or so I thought. I drove home and found a message on my machine from Rosemary. The condensed, repeatable version was that she'd found out about her car.

From the police.

Right before they put her in a line-up with a bunch of hookers.

Since I lacked the skills of a fugitive and it wasn't Rosemary's fault she was my twin, I decided to turn myself in. It had nothing to do with the fact that it would be safer for me to be in jail now that she knew about her car.

In the police station I approached the desk, but before I

could ask about Rosemary, I heard a familiar voice behind me.

"Miss Stanley?" I turned to find Drum's dad, Detective Dillion looking at me, his signature suspicious expression in place. "Is something wrong?"

"Maybe." The look in his eyes killed any urge I might have to confess. "My sister's here. Somewhere."

"Really."

I didn't like the way he said it, but I had no choice but to follow him through two doors. Far too quickly I found myself looking at my sister. At least I had police protection. I looked at said protection. Their mutually shocked expressions, made me realize I'd be a fool to count on them for anything until they had time to assimilate our twin-ness.

Rosemary's fingers curled into claws. She started toward me.

Time to play the guilt card. "So, how was your date with Mike?"

An interrogation room in a police station is not a good place to be left alone with your thoughts. Dillion and his partner Willis, whose fish-like visage made me itch to sketch him, had finally taken Rosemary away to arrange her release, leaving me to ponder my situation.

The pondering was not particularly fruitful. I didn't know if asking for a lawyer would make me look more guilty or if a strip search would be better or worse than the yearly pelvic exam?

In the distance I heard Rosemary go ballistic again. Something about her car. I probably shouldn't count on her as a character witness.

I shifted on the hard chair, wishing for something to fill the void besides my mouse-on-a-wheel thoughts. Since illustration is my usual response to stress, I produced a battered sketch book and a piece of pencil from the deep depths of my purse. A few swift strokes and Cochran appeared on the page wearing prison stripes. I added tiny caricatures of Willis and Dillon doing a Russian dance on either side of him. Willis was a fish, of course. Dillon was a dog, a yippy, dust-mop dog.

Dillon. I paused and frowned into the distance. He was, I was sure, my enemy. Wait until he found out I'm sort of dating his son. I'd probably never get out of jail.

Jail. How had I got into this mess? My fingers moved as my thoughts roamed back to the how. Dates, deaths and car chases tumbled together. Had I really seen the round-headed man at the Tandoor? And how much should I tell the cops about Kel?

Not that I had that much to tell—

The door opened suddenly. I jumped, spilling pad and pencil onto the floor. The pencil rolled across the uneven linoleum floor and came to rest against Dillon's shoe.

"Sorry." I crouched to retrieve my stuff. Willis bent to help me and our heads collided. "Aaugh! I didn't mean to assault you!"

He grinned and scooped my pad out from under my hand. "Try to relax, Miss Stanley. We're not ogres."

I looked past him to Dillon. He didn't look like he agreed with his partner. Then he stepped on my pencil.

"Sorry." He picked up the pieces and tossed them onto the table. Both pieces rolled into an indentation in the surface on one side. It looked like it was from beating heads there. A tiny, sympathetic ache formed around my eyes, then fanned out along my forehead.

"You're an artist?" Willis flipped casually through my sketch pad.

"Sort of." I twitched as he got closer and closer to the page with the sketch I'd just done of him.

"I've seen this bug before." He looked up. "You the one does the cockroach books?"

"Yes." Was this going to help or hurt my cause?

"My sister's kids love your books. I don't suppose you'd autograph one of these for them?"

What? Was I going to say no to a cop?

"Sure." I reached for the book. Dillon cleared his throat ominously. "Was that wrong? I'm not trying to bribe him. Really. I'm a law abiding person. I'm probably the most law abiding person you've ever arrested. I've never even gone in an out door or taken tags off my pillows!"

Dillon sighed. "You read mysteries, don't you?"

"Yes, but I can stop anytime."

"How about this one?" Willis held up the page I'd just done. In center place, larger than the rest, was my roach with he and Dillon doing their dance. "I think they'd like this one. This one kind of looks like you, Dillon."

He stopped, his stocky, fish-shaped body going all stiff.

Law suit time.

I snatched the sketchbook from him and slammed it shut. "I'm sorry. That's part of a work in progress."

"Can we get down to business?" Dillon paced impatiently across the narrow room, his hands shoved in the pockets of his suit pants. His tie was listing toward his left ear. I got the feeling he blamed me for all of it.

"Of course." I sat down and looked cooperatively at Willis. He didn't look as friendly as before. A distraction was clearly in order. "I'm surprised you got onto my sister so quickly."

"We're not quite as incompetent as the media like to make out," Dillon snapped.

"And when she was identified in the line-up—" Willis

shrugged, settling into a chair facing me.

"The man with the dust-mop dog. I knew it. His dog was pooing on someone's lawn, you know."

"This will take less time if you'll wait until we ask you questions," Willis said, amusement creeping back into his eyes.

Dillon leaned toward me again. "Let's start with the bullet holes in your sister's car. Where they came from? Why you were seen speeding from the scene of Carter's murder?"

"Uh, because I didn't want to get shot?"

Dillon slammed his hands against the table. "Don't mess with me!"

I cowered in my cower-resistant seat. "I'm not! You don't have to scare me into spilling my guts. I'll spill them without the act."

I looked at Willis, then Dillon. They looked confused.

"What act?" Willis finally asked.

"Good cop, bad cop." They looked at each other, then me again. I hastened to reassure them. "Don't feel bad. You do it very well. It's just that I was expecting it. I can pretend I don't notice if you want."

Willis gave a half laugh, half snort and rested his arms on the seat back. "You're a very, unusual woman, Miss Stanley."

"Oh no. I'm hopelessly ordinary. That's what makes this whole thing so weird!"

"Don't you think its stretching things a bit to call murder weird?" Dillon asked, pacing around to loom over me.

"Murder isn't exactly normal," I felt the need to point out.

Dillon looked inclined to puff up again, but Willis laughed and said, "Can it, Ken. Miss Stanley is cooperating. You can badger our next witness."

With an air of forbearance, Dillon hooked a chair with his

foot and straddled it like a rebellious teenager. I gave him a "teacher look," which seemed to disconcert him. Satisfied, I looked helpfully at Willis.

Willis' lips twitched, but all he said was, "Let's take it from the top. Why did Carter's killer shoot at you?"

I explained about the choir practice and Mrs. MacPhearson while Dillon beat an impatient tattoo on the floor with his foot. When I paused for breath, he jumped on me with, "The Carter house isn't on your way home, Miss Stanley."

"I know. I was thinking, you see." I leaned forward and rested my elbows on the table. "I'm trying to get out of bugs and into romance novels, but it's not as easy as some people think it is. I was mulling my book and not watching where I was going. And when I stopped, I realized I was lost, well, not exactly lost, but not sure where I was. That's when I drove by her house." I shrugged. "It was just a coincidence."

"A coincidence?" Dillon fixed me with an official glare. "Want to hear another coincidence?" I had a feeling I didn't, but he didn't wait for my assent to tell me, "Paul Mitchell was killed with the same gun that killed Carter."

"Two murders in two days is pushing the coincidence envelope pretty far," Willis added.

"The same gun?" I sagged back. Maybe it had been the round-headed man I saw in the parking lot? This was not good. "This really isn't my week."

"Apparently Carter volunteered at a youth center that helped teens get off drugs," Willis said. "We found drugs on Mitchell's body—"

"But it couldn't be drugs." I turned to Dillon. "According to your son, Paul Mitchell was a major straight arrow kid. No way he'd be using the stuff."

"My son?" Dillon began, puffing up again, but the door

opened abruptly. Naturally we all looked. In the opening I saw yet another cop. Behind him were two men in suits.

"What's up?" Willis stood up, his body going oddly tense at the sudden interruption.

"They're here for Miss Stanley."

"What?" Dillon jumped up. "We're not through with her yet."

The cop shrugged. "Their paperwork is in order. She belongs to them now."

She? Who? Me?

The cop left, leaving the identical suits. It wasn't just their conservative gray suits, white shirts, or proper ties that matched. Their blank, cool faces were almost identical, too. Only their hair was different, one light and one dark.

A mouth moved in the face of the light-haired guy, exposing a perfectly straight line of white teeth. "Will you please come with us, Miss Stanley?"

I clutched my purse to my chest, too shocked for words.

Willis had plenty to say. "She's our witness! You can't waltz in here and take her! Not till we've finished getting her statement!"

Like identical marionettes they pulled open their jackets, extracted matching leather wallets and flipped them open. Dillon took a hard look, then wheeled angrily away.

"You damn spooks think you can do whatever you want!"

Willis' face was tight with rage. "What possible interest could the CIA have in the murder of a math teacher in the suburbs?"

"I'm afraid we're not at liberty to answer questions," the dark-haired partner spoke this time.

Dillon slammed his hands down on the table, catching the point of my broken pencil and sending it sailing through the air. "You're out of your jurisdiction! This is our case!"

The pencil hit the wall, then floor, where it rolled back between Dillon's feet.

Neither spook reacted. Light hair said, "It's still your case. You'll just have to solve it without Miss Stanley. Like the man said, she's ours now. So back off."

They closed in on either side of me, grabbed my arms, and swept me out the door and down the hall. There was one brief check to our exit. A uniformed officer approached me holding up a familiar looking glue gun.

"Miss Stanley? I think this is your sister's. We forgot to give it to her when she reclaimed her personal items."

I recognized Rosemary's monogram on the side. She loved that glue gun almost as much as her car. Still gripped by suits, I signed something, took the gun and shoved it in my purse. The spooks started us toward the exit again, my dragging feet barely brushing the floor, the glue gun cord slapping against my legs.

"It's all right, Miss Stanley. Trust us," dark hair said.

Trust the CIA? I don't think so.

Outside a long, dark limo waited. They stuffed me in it with insulting ease. I landed untidily in a lap. A familiar smell teased my nostrils. I didn't even have to look. But of course I did.

Kelvin Kapone.

Not a private investigator. A spy.

Darn his deceitful, smiling self.

Chapter Twelve

"Would you believe me if I said I'm not a spy?"

"No." I slid untidily onto the seat next to him. "Why should I believe anything you say? You told me you were a private detective."

"You told me I was a private detective."

"You agreed with me!"

"I didn't disagree with you. There's a difference."

"Only to a spook!" I straightened as much as I could in the soft, deep seat and looked haughtily out the window.

"And what would you have done if I'd told you I was CIA?"

I shrugged to indicate my total lack of interest in him or his lies. And then made the mistake of looking at him to see how he liked the cold shoulder.

The back seat of the limo closed us in a dim intimacy that put interesting shadows across his clean cut face and high-lighted his bright, white smile. He smelled of soap and after-shave, the expensive kind. His eyes held a nice mix of remorse and an engaging invitation to freely forgive, to come bask again in their warm blue light.

"I wouldn't have believed you," I admitted, giving him a dark look. "Why would I expect James Bond to dive through my sunroof in the suburbs?"

He looked penitent, though his eyes quickly lost the re-morse and filled with wicked humor. "If it makes you feel any better, I was being chased on my own time. I went there because my mother asked me to."

"Your mother? Are spies allowed to have mothers?"

"If we don't have one, then one is issued to us."

How could he keep his face so serious, while his eyes laughed so outrageously?

"If I'd known . . ." I began.

"You didn't need to know."

I looked up at that. "Oh really? And now I do?"

"Let's just say the local police don't need to know." Then he had the nerve to grin at me.

It was practically atomic in intensity and stirred up all the things I shouldn't be feeling. This guy was totally out of my league. I was a Baptist children's book author. He was a CIA agent. End of story. So why did my lips curve in a smile loaded with idiocy? I shook away idiocy and asked, "How did you know I was at the police station?"

"Would you believe, we have our ways?"

I stared at him for a full minute before it hit me. I'm slow, but I get there eventually if I have enough really obvious clues.

"You're—you're having me followed, aren't you?"

"You can ID a killer, Bel. Was I supposed to let you wander around unprotected?"

Men. They always insist on being logical. The idea of being followed around when I didn't know it, made me feel completely illogical. What if I'd done something I didn't want the CIA to know about? Like . . . like . . . I couldn't think of anything I could do that would even interest them, so I said, "If he'd seen me, wouldn't he have tried to kill me by now? I mean, we were both at the Tandoor Club last night and no one's tried to kill me. Except Rosemary."

"I'd prefer not to wait until it's too late. You saved my life,

Bel." He leaned close and ran a gentle finger along my cheek, sending chills down to my toes. "I'd like to return the favor."

I couldn't breath. He was too close and his eyes so sincerely blue, how could I deny him anything?

"Well," I licked my lips and offered grudgingly, "Okay, you can save my life. But I want it on the record that I don't like being followed without my consent."

"We try to keep everything off the record."

I had to smile then. "Spook."

He grinned again, with the shameless brass of a man who knew he'd just got his way. Since I was used to not getting my way, I asked without angst, "What do you want me to do?"

"How much did they get out of you before my men got there?"

I shrugged. "Not much. We were past Mrs. MacPhearson and the flu but just coming up on you and the round-headed man." I frowned. "Isn't it kind of mean to not let them know who the major suspect is?"

"For the time being, the fewer people who know about you the better. Police stations are notorious for leaks."

"Unlike the CIA."

He pretended not to hear. "I'd like to keep you under wraps until I can find out why Mrs. Carter called me instead of the police."

"Oh. Did she know? That you're a spy, I mean?"

"I'm not a spy. I'm an agent," he said, with obvious pride, "trying to protect my country."

Whoa, an idealistic spook? Wasn't that a contradiction in terms? Sure as tooting it shouldn't make me feel all warm and fuzzy. Too bad what I shouldn't feel didn't seem to stop me from feeling it.

In a move that seemed too natural, he shifted, resting his arm on the seat behind my head. He wasn't touching me, but

I didn't need fully body contact to reach volcanic.

Enclosed in a field of warmth that was both reassuring and scary, I had to fight an unworthy compulsion to nestle in against him and play helpless female. A small, satisfied smile played with the edges of his mouth. I briefly let myself get side-tracked remembering what it had felt like to have that mouth moving on mine. I might have let the volcano erupt if it weren't for his very apparent, total lack of repentance.

I gave him my wide-eyed innocent look and asked, "So what have you found out about Mrs. Carter's death that the police haven't?"

His gaze shifted just off the right of mine. "We're still analyzing the data obtained from her purse."

I choked.

"What?" He sounded nicely defensive.

"Why don't you just admit you don't have a clue?"

"When I signed on with the CIA I had to promise I would never do that." He looked perfectly serious, except for a twinkle at the back of his eyes.

I shook my head. A CIA agent with a sense of humor. Wasn't that also a contradiction in terms? Though a very nice contradiction. Definitely a dangerous man.

"You know the police think it's drug related?"

"Elspeth Carter?" Kel shook his head. "Drugs? I don't believe it. She was completely opposed to drugs."

"Not her. The boy, Paul Mitchell. They were killed with the same gun, you know. They told me at the police station."

"What?" Kel frowned. It didn't mar his looks one bit. "That doesn't feel right. I knew she did some work in drug prevention, but it makes no sense."

"I don't know about that, but I know that Paul's friends say he wasn't the type to use. He was with the Guard, shipping out to the Gulf soon. A real stand-up kind of guy and squeaky clean."

He ran a hand into his hair, making that question mark clump fall endearingly onto his forehead. I wanted to smooth it back, but lacked permission. And the nerve.

"Everything about this case is squeaky clean," Kel said, his frown deepening.

"Except the murders."

We both fell silent. He stared into the distance, while I tried not to stare at him. He sat there positively radiating idealism. Which was probably what had prompted me to help him.

Baptists are particularly susceptible to idealism.

I frowned. Wasn't my religion supposed to make me immune to his long, lean body and the heady scent of male after-shave? Or at least help temptation get thee behind me? I took another peek and temptation stayed right in my face. Obviously my principles needed some help. It seemed like a good idea to stop thinking and start talking.

"Where are we going?"

"Hmm?" He looked up, then said with an air of putting things temporarily away, "The impound lot to pick up your sister's car. There's really no reason for them to hold it, so I applied a little pressure to have it released."

"You may have saved my life. If I bring back her baby maybe Rosemary will only beat me senseless."

"Do you have time for some lunch?"

I felt a little thrill, until he added, "I'd like you to look through some mug books for your round-headed man. The sooner the killer is identified and arrested, the sooner the CIA can quit tailing you against your will."

"Oh." That didn't sound as appealing as it should have. When they got their man, would this particular CIA guy quit tailing me? Duh. Of course. I looked away and gave a tiny shrug. "Sure."

The street passed without me seeing it. Even a big "SALE" sign in a dress shop window caused no more than a flicker of interest. I could feel him looking at me and wanted to tell him to stop it. Instead I twisted the strap of my purse until it left a red mark across my hand. His hand covered mine, stopping the attempted self-mutilation.

"Mexican okay? I know this good place close to the impound lot."

"Sounds fine." Despite a stern, mental admonition, my gaze slid his way and ran smack into his. I don't know if he started to lean towards me, or the car turning the corner leaned him towards me. I just know he was incoming and I was outgoing. Before we could lip lock, the car stopped with an un-limousine-like jerk. The suits slid smoothly out each side and pulled open the doors, flooding the cozy, dim interior with harsh light and the real world.

"Impound lot," Kel said.

Did he sound regretful? I wasn't unbiased enough to judge.

I reined in my lips and started to slide out. I don't know if lust made me clumsy or careless. Probably both. My foot caught on something under the seat. Launching me into an ungraceful nose dive out the door. Lucky for me the suit on my side had good reflexes. Too bad he was short the extra arm to catch my purse.

A mini eruption of contents sprayed out onto the pavement. Crumpled, dirty papers fluttered. Useless sundries rolled in ten different directions. A bedraggled sanitary napkin landed at the suit's feet, accompanied by a shower of tiny, green breath mints. And that was just the small stuff.

He had me around the waist, while I tried to untangle my

feet from the car and simultaneously grab at flying objects. I succeeded only in spreading them further, not to mention putting my rescue in peril. Suit number two rushed to our aid just in time to become the unhappy recipient of several tampons.

Kel kept his distance until the dust and my belongings settled. Then he quietly started to gather up everything within his reach, his face carefully expressionless.

When he wasn't looking I kicked an unwrapped tampon under the car. Had I really thought a spit rainbow the worst blow life could inflict?

I opened the bag's maw and stoically received my belongings as they were proffered. The pocketbook with the tattered edges, the map of New Orleans, the ceramic crawfish, a three year old date book (empty), the brush with no bristles, and the business card case with the Junior Mint still stuck to it. The last thing Kel handed me was the glue gun.

"My sister's," I muttered. "She likes to glue things."

"Do you think that's everything?"

Right. Like I'd know that. I smiled brightly, taking care to avoid eye contact. "Of course."

There was this strange, insistent buzzing from the bowels of the limo and one of the suits peeled off to silence it, leaving me to reinsert the glue gun under the gaze of only two incredulous men.

"Sir?"

Kel looked away. "What?"

"That was Edwards. Says PT-PAC looks clean."

"Right. Tell him I'll see him at the dog and pony show this afternoon." Kel turned back to me as the suits faded into the limo, which pulled away with a relieved purr.

"Dog and pony show? You a judge?"

Kel smiled and shook his head. "It's a meeting."

"Oh. Right." Spy talk. No wonder our country was in trouble.

"Shall we get your sister's car?"

I'd humiliated myself enough for now, so I nodded. I was also too cowed by the purse incident to do more than murmur assent when Kel offered to drive.

We pulled out into traffic. Eager for a change of subject, I asked, "Is that Mrs. Carter's PAC your guy was talking about?"

Kel nodded, his eyes on the rear view mirror as he moved over a lane. "It was her pride and joy. The night she died, she attended a meeting of the board."

"And you think her death had something to do with that?" From pride and joy to death in the board room? It was a stretch, in my opinion, even for the CIA.

"It's not likely. But she did mention being worried about one of her projects." He shrugged. "Though I can't imagine anyone transgressing under her eagle eye."

"Know that from experience, do you?"

"Well . . ." He grinned at me, then took the car smoothly round a corner, the motor purring with contentment.

I basked in the lingering glow of his smile. Pity he had to watch the road so closely.

It was weird to be back in Rosemary's car with him. Even weirder to think I'd wandered into some real-life spy flick, complete with bodies, mysteries, and a handsome hero. Too bad there was only me to play the heroine part. Just because he wasn't married, didn't mean he didn't have a significant other tucked away somewhere.

I sighed. Oh well, I'd have my memories.

He shifted in his seat and grimaced like it hurt.

"Are you all right? You're pretty active for a guy with a bullet hole in his side."

He stopped at a light with no sign of impatience. "It's just a scratch."

Sub-text: Real men don't feel pain.

"I guess you have to get used to bullet wounds."

He chuckled. "It's not all that dangerous." He passed through the light and pulled into a space in front of a row of stores.

"If we common people have misconceptions about the CIA, it's because the CIA likes it that way."

"Maybe." He turned off the car and towards me, resting his arm along the seat back behind my head.

The car immediately shrunk. I shifted nervously. Stared at the restaurant's façade, then let my gaze homing pigeon back to him. "This the place?"

He nodded. "Look okay?"

"Yeah." I wasn't talking about the restaurant.

He knew it. His eyes heated up as he ran his finger lightly down the side of my neck. "Good."

I was sure he was going to kiss me, but he got out and slammed the door. I watched him pace around the car, wondering what kind of spy softened a lady up, then failed to follow through and kiss her? James Bond would be very disappointed in him.

He opened my door and helped me out. We were so close, I could have inhaled him, if I could have breathed. If he didn't kiss me this time . . .

He started to, I think. Distantly, I heard the sound of a car accelerating too fast. Instead he looked away. I followed his lead and saw the green minivan careening towards us, an assault weapon poking out the window.

Fortunately his reflexes were faster than mine. I was still registering shock, when he shoved me to the pavement behind the Mercedes. Seconds later the shooting started. For a brief eternity, my face was pushed into cold concrete with Kel's body covering mine while all hell broke loose above us. As abruptly as it started, the shooting stopped. The diminishing shriek of tires faded into cries of fear and outrage.

The air was filled with the acrid smell of cordite. Over Kel's shoulder I saw shattered glass and twisted metal where Rosemary's car used to be.

"You should have let them shoot me," I told him.

Sirens drowned out people noise. Kel helped me up, brushed the glass off my clothes and hair, had someone bring me a chair and a glass of water. I sat and sipped, once more surrounded by policemen and flashing lights. That it was happening in the bright light of midday didn't make it feel any more real than the last time.

I let it all pass over and around me as I stared glumly at the car's remains, only half listening as Kel talked to Willis about the shooting.

"So, Miss Stanley," I looked up into Dillon's sardonic face, "what you gonna do for your next trick?"

I looked at Rosemary's car. "Disappear?"

Four hours, six feet of mug books, and one police artist later, I think everyone wished I had disappeared.

"How's this, Miss Stanley?" the artist asked for the umpteenth time. I looked at the much erased sketch for a moment, then at the tired artist. "It's very nice."

"But does it look like the man you saw?" If he'd been six instead of twenty-six, I'd have said he was whining.

Behind him Willis was banging his head lightly, rhythmically, against the wall. Kel was stretched out in a chair, his hands clasped behind his head as he studied the ceiling. Dillon paced between us like a caged lion.

"No . . ."

Their frustrated sighs almost blew me out the door. I had to do something before they turned ugly. I took the sketch book and pencil.

"May I?" Without waiting for his answer, I flipped to a clean page and started to fill it with broad strokes. It was easy. The round-headed man's visage was burned in my memory. Maybe sketching him would exorcise it.

"You—you're—you can—why?" the artist sputtered.

I looked up. "They all knew I could."

There was this pregnant pause, then the three of them sputtered out a defensive chorus, "She draws cockroaches—not people—"

"There." I made a couple of minute adjustments, gave a final shudder, and handed the pad back to its frustrated owner. "That's him."

They all huddled over the sketch.

"It's a caricature," Willis said.

I wondered how many of my tax dollars had gone into training him?

"A damn good one," Kel murmured, giving me a quick, tired smile that made up for everything.

"A caricature, but still recognizable," Dillon said, something that was almost pleasure forming on his face. "In fact, I think I've seen him somewhere before."

"I don't know," Willis said. "Maybe we ought to wait, try to get a better picture to put on the wire."

"Better than what? We'll have him in custody inside thirty-six hours." Dillon headed for the door with the sketch in hand.

I faded gratefully into the woodwork as they launched into law enforcement mode. With my eyes closed, my thoughts drifted, unfocused, unstructured, something hovering at the back of my mind. Something important, waiting patiently for recognition—

—don't want anyone else to know you saw him—

—police stations are notoriously leaky places—

I felt a chill spreading through me despite the over-heated room. I was too tired to think straight. I shouldn't go there.

—Kel saved my life—

—he couldn't—

—not and kiss like that—

—but how did the round-headed man know—

—Kel. Kel was the only one who knew—

No, he couldn't, wouldn't—a pounding in my temples kept time with the insistent, unanswerable question, if not Kel, then who?

Who else had known where we were, where we were going? He got shot at, too, I wailed inside my head. Bad guys turn on each other, my head shot back.

I had to get out of here. I needed time, space to think, away from him. I needed facts, not feelings to tell me whether Kel wanted to kiss me—or kill me. I needed—my mother.

That's how desperate I was.

At the end of the narrow hall, I spotted an exit sign and headed for it. No one noticed. Outside it was cold and gray, like I felt inside. Rosemary had taken my car. Hers was a skeleton of its former self. A bus paused at a corner, people filing on. I could do that and did, dropping into a seat just before my legs gave out.

The bus jerked forward as Kel burst out the door. I cowered in my seat, not daring to look back until we turned the corner and he was lost to sight.

If I cried on the way home, it was no one's business but mine.

Chapter Thirteen

Rosemary didn't kill me when I walked through the door. I think she thought I was already dead. Or maybe our mother standing there crimped her style.

"My car?" Rosemary asked.

I burst into tears. My mother rose to the occasion, folding me into her arms despite the grit and grime of being drive-by shot at. I was too tired to cry long. My mother mopped me up, question marks becoming prominent in her fine eyes when Rosemary brought me the telephone.

"Bel?" Kel's voice in my ear was as heady as a New Orleans pastry. "You made it safely home, then?"

Tiny tentacles of warmth began to dispel the chill in my bones at the relief in his voice.

"Why did you run out on me?"

"You seemed busy . . . and I was really tired." Questions tried to break through exhaustion. Questions I couldn't ask. My mother was standing there. Besides, I might not like the answers.

"I'm really sorry," he said.

For involving me in a life threatening situation or for needing to kill me, I wondered.

"I have my men watching your house. You'll be safe until we find this guy."

Would I? I really wanted to feel safe again.

"Thank you. Really. I appreciate it." Was I thanking my

hero? Or my enemy? I was too tired to care anymore. He rang off and I let the arm holding the telephone drop to my side. My mother and my sister stared at me. "I'm going to bed."

Amazingly neither of them tried to stop me. I was too tired not to sleep, but my dreams prominently featured the round-headed man in his green van. I finally gave in and woke up. Morning was better than this kind of sleep. And I didn't want to be late for my appointment to autograph cockroach butts.

When I'd done what I could to mitigate the ravages to my person, I grabbed my purse and headed for my car. Rosemary had parked it out front, right across from the two agents assigned to guard me. Keeping a wary eye on them in the rear view mirror, I steered a course for the nearest Burger King where I ordered a six pack of muffins to clear the angst from my head. My protectors followed me inside, looking silly and sinister as they sat nearby, still wearing sunglasses and sipping orange juice from little cartons.

No wonder it was hard to take the CIA seriously.

I lost them when I went in the convention center. I had a pass to the convention floor and they didn't. Since I was early, I took my time.

The exhibits were varied and interesting. My sketch fingers started to itch. Then I saw this huge, sand sculpture in the middle of the floor. Sculptors were still busy shaping the sand into a composition of books, kids, and monsters. And I thought roaches were tough to work with.

I had to get this down. I dug through my purse for my sketch pad. Then dug through again. The only thing I found there was a lot of junk and Rosemary's glue gun. Where was it? Last time I'd had it had been . . . the police station. Then I'd spewed all the contents of my purse getting out of the CIA limo. Had it been overlooked inside the limo or on the ground under the limo? I'd have to ask Kel, but didn't know what to hope for. I hated to lose the sketches I'd made, but did I really want Kel to know more about me than he already did? Looking in my sketch book was tantamount to reading someone else's diary.

I was so bummed, I almost didn't see the exhibit for PT-PAC, the late Mrs. Carter's committee. Curious, I strolled over to a woman arranging brochures. She looked a little wan around the edges, her eyes red-rimmed and tired, but she managed a semi-smile for me as I walked up to her.

"Would you like to sign our petition?"

"Well, if I agree with you, I guess I could." I'd made the mistake of signing something I didn't agree with one other time in my life, which was the main reason I was on my way to sign roach tushes.

She launched into a little spiel about the group, how their main focus was improving education, but because they kept running up against the special interest lock on Congress they had decided to focus on getting term limitations and line item veto for the President. She handed me a wad of pamphlets as she spoke. Of course I signed. Who wasn't against Congress?

I added her stuff to the mess in my purse, then asked, hesitantly, "I guess Mrs. Carter's death isn't going to disband the group?"

Tears welled, then spilled from her eyes. She didn't ask how, just murmured. "It's such a horrible thing. And then Paul, too . . ." her voice broke and she turned away.

"Paul Mitchell was part of your group, too?" She nodded. "How awful!" And what a weird coincidence. I could feel my dormant sleuth gland start to stir. Luckily I got interrupted.

"Stan! How charming to run into you again." It was Flynn Kenyon again. Another weird coincidence. Hadn't seen him for months and now I'd run into him twice in as many days. He had a Pt-PAC button pinned to the lapel of his Armani suit and looked more salvation salesman-ish than usual.

"I didn't realize you were involved in this, too. Am I the only person I know who isn't?" I asked.

He smiled whitely. "You'd be surprised who is." He looked at his watch. "You'll have to excuse me. I have a meeting across town I have to attend."

I watched his tall figure retreat through the crowd, turned to leave and slammed into a chest. Hands gripped my arms, I looked up, half expecting Kel, but the after shave wasn't right. It smelled more like Dag.

Looked like him, too.

"Great." I jerked free of his hold.

"What a pleasant encounter, darling Isabel. See I didn't confuse you this time." He glanced around. "No big boyfriend in tow?"

"No. You don't have to be afraid."

"I'm never afraid, darling, just cautious. Have you ever wondered why you're so anxious to avoid me?"

"No, Dag. I know why I'm so anxious to avoid you. You make me sick." I showed him a stiff back as I marched away.

Nasty, but he'd accomplished something a shower and a six pack of muffins hadn't. He'd got my blood moving.

Boiling actually.

My editor looked up as I approached. Small and stocky, Marion looked brisk even when seated behind a table.

"Stan?" Her brows rose slowly as she took in my appearance. "You look—"

"Like hell. I know. You're lucky I made it. Just give me a pen and point me toward the bug butts."

She did as requested. "Do I hope that someday you'll explain why you look like that?"

"Just watch for me on CNN."

She sighed. "You'll do anything to get out of autographing books, won't you?"

"Too bloody right," I snapped, picking up the pen and pulling the first poster butt toward me.

The Dag induced energy surge faded far too quickly. I signed steadily for a small eternity and finally the line decreased to a small trickle, then stopped altogether. I stretched my tired hand and gave Marion a piteous look.

"Can I take a break?"

"Fifteen more minutes. How bad can it be?"

Before I could tell her, the table shook as a pile of books were dropped in front of me. I let my gaze rise slowly up the stack of books to a large woman with a gold front tooth.

"Oh, Miss Stanley! I can't tell you how excited I am to meet you! My class just loves your books!"

"I'm glad." If they liked them so much, why was she returning all of them?

"I told them I just knew you'd autograph their books for them. I had them put a little slip inside with their name and the inscription they'd like. If you don't mind?"

"Of course she doesn't mind." Marion gave me a you'd-better-not-mind look.

"Of course I don't mind." I opened the first book and picked up the white slip tucked inside. "To Michael, my main man. From your hot, hot mama. Uh, what grade is it you teach?"

"Remedial high schoolers."

I turned to give Marion a look that would have killed her on the spot if she hadn't taken the opportunity to book out of there.

The coward.

I was on the way back from my long delayed bathroom

break when I saw the round-headed man standing next to the sand sculpture, pretending to read some fliers while he cast furtive looks around. He was older than he'd looked in the dark, probably in his late forties or early fifties, and wearing a western-cut polyester suit that highlighted his figure flaws, particularly the place where stomach spill hid his belt. His pointed feet were shoved into cowboy boots and turned out, remarkably like the cartoon character I'd sketched him as. Only he wasn't a cartoon.

He was a killer.

And he was looking for me.

He looked up and found me. He started toward me when something low and gray, hit him dead center. Cowboy and spy sprawled into the sand sculpture. Grappling awkwardly, the two men, one round, and one straight, rolled through a sand child before crashing to the floor. A cascade of sand followed them down as a week's worth of sculpting dissolved under the hands of startled workers.

Above their grunts and groans and the gasps of onlookers, I heard the shrill wail of whistles. Two security guards rushed onto the scene and pushed their way through the crowd that quickly formed around the struggling figures.

For a minute it was a game of Twister without the mat as the guards tried to drag my suit off the round-headed man. All of them were slipping and sliding on the sand. None of them looked like they were enjoying it.

Then the four men broke apart. The round-headed man was free and furious. He shook sand from his scant hair and glared around. In a classic case of clueless, the two guards jumped my suit.

I didn't wait to see more. I took off, running right out of my high heeled shoes. My heavy purse banged rhythmically against my side as I scampered between exhibits and people. I contemplated off-loading it, but it was the only thing I had that remotely resembled a weapon. Besides, inside it was a driver's license picture that was actually decent. They'd have to pry that from my cold, dead fingers.

I dashed and dodged, riding a wave of panic that swept away any rational thought. When I saw the double doors to one side, I made a sharp right, slid across the cement floor and crashed into them. Jerked one open and slid through.

I knew right away I'd made a bad choice, but my body was still running ahead of my brain. It just kept fleeing down the hallway, leaving behind the safety of bright lights and the comforting sounds of potential eye witnesses.

There was no cover in the hallway, so I picked up the pace a bit, went round a corner and almost launched myself down a stairway. Only by grabbing the iron rail as I went by, did I change a header down the stairs into a body slam into a brick wall.

This gave my brain a minute to catch up with my body.

The stairs marched down into a murky, half lit world rumbling with the muted sound of machinery. My body started to listen to my brain screaming caution, until my ears heard the door open and the distinctive snap of cowboy boots on cement.

Instinct took over again.

My stocking feet were soundless against the steps, my brain screaming at me to run, as I plunged recklessly down into the bowels of the physical plant. A brief landing at the bottom, a skid, then I was running down a dark passage like a Gothic heroine, my purse and braid streaming behind. On either side rose huge, dark shapes, groaning monster inhabitants of this nether world.

I kept turning down passages, always choosing the darker, until I ran out of steam and passages and into a brick wall. My chest heaved with fright and the need for air. I slid to the floor with my back against the wall. As my breathing gradually evened out, I realized the thump, thump, thump I thought was my heart was actually cowboy boots against the cement floor coming directly toward me.

Chapter Fourteen

I pressed back into the small space under a kind of boiler as a scream tried to crawl up and out my throat. Fear put a choke hold on said throat when a dark figure passed, then paused, the roundness of his head clearly visible against the dim overhead bulb.

He waited, his head bent in a listening attitude while light found and lit a dull gleam in the weapon he carried. I closed my eyes, so he wouldn't see my whites and shoot. That's when I heard more footsteps.

Rescue or an accomplice?

I had to peek. The round-headed man tensed, reached up and loosened the bulb overhead, then stepped back into my shadows.

He was so close I could smell his noxious after-shave mixed with acrid sweat. What came first, I wondered, the bad taste, then bad guy or the bad guy, then bad taste?

Not my finest hour, I'll admit, but the sheer terror, followed by shallow thought made me realize I could still think.

While I had my mini-epiphany, whoever was approaching came into the round-headed guy's range. He said, in this growly, bad-guy voice, "Hold it right there, bitch."

An understandable error, given the light. I didn't know who it was, but I couldn't sit here and let someone get shot for me.

If only I had a gun.

Wait. I did have a gun. Of sorts.

I eased my hand in my purse and felt through the debris until I found the handle of Rosemary's glue gun.

"You shoulda kept pretending you didn't know anything, doll. Mighta stayed alive. Let's see some hands."

The amazing thing was that he could see at all. I'd had time for my eyes to adjust to the dark and I could barely see his round-headed outline against the general murk.

Still, even a mental midget would have to notice the difference between a female victim and what I suspected was a CIA suit.

I pulled the glue gun clear of the purse.

"That's it, get those hands up nice and high. And let's have your purse. I need that picture you made of me."

What? This guy wasn't just evil, he was stupid. Didn't he know the police had that picture?

I left my purse on the floor and rose slowly, gripping the glue gun with both hands, the way they did it in the movies.

The round-headed man didn't move. All of his little brain was directed to where he thought I was. I took a steadying breath. Then jammed the glue gun into his fleshy back as hard as I could.

"Don't move, dirt bag!" I growled trying to sound deep and official. "Lose the piece!"

He started, then said, "I have the bitch in my sights, spook. Now mebbe you better drop your heater before I do her."

With a clarity honed by adrenaline, I knew what to do. I slid the gun down his back until the glue gun was digging into his fat behind.

"Only way you have me in your sights, is if your eyes are in your ass with your brain, idiot. Now drop that gun before I make you into a freaking soprano!"

I gave him a good, hard jab to press home my point.

"Now, lady," his voice spontaneously rose a couple of octaves, "don't get your drawers in a twist! See," he extended his arms, the gun swinging lightly from his fat finger and thumb, "see, I'm putting it down. Just stay calm."

"Don't tell me to stay calm. It makes me nervous. Did I mention this has a hair trigger?" It wasn't a lie. Rosemary had bought top of the line. This baby could produce a thin line of glue if you just thought you wanted it to. "Put the gun down and kick it toward the spook before I do something you'll regret!"

I gave him another jab. It felt good. Maybe I should have been a cop. Or a spook.

"Okay! Okay!"

He bent to lay the gun down. The suit had his gun up, peering into our dark passage. Then another suit called out.

It was just the distraction the round-headed man was waiting for. He elbowed me. My breath woofed out. He lunged forward and applied one of those shoulder butts football players do to the suit's solar plexus. His breath woofed out, too.

Gamely the suit made a grab for the round-headed man, got a knee to the jaw for his trouble and went down.

Round head made a grab for his gun, but I saw that one coming and kicked it into the shadows.

"We're here! Help!" Self-defense 101. Make a lot of noise.

I made more noise and the round-headed man staggered forward, his cowboy boots skidding against the floor for several dancing steps, then he got his footing and scampered down the passage, the frantic echo of his footsteps gradually fading away.

"You all right, Miss Stanley?" The suit helped me to my feet.

I did a little shimmy. It hurt, but no pain that was out of the ordinary. "Yeah, I'm okay."

He brought out a little flash light and shined it around, then pointed it at the glue gun. "You should've shot him."

"I couldn't." I held it up, so that he could see the cord dangling from the butt. "It wasn't plugged in."

He stared at the gun, incredulity breaking out all over his face. "Holy shit."

They assigned me some new suits because my old ones were "mopping up" at the convention center. The new guys tried but failed to look identical. One was tall and round, the other short and thin.

As I drove home, I realized the incident had left more questions than it answered. How had round head found out I could ID him or that I was at the convention center?

The evidence was stacking up against Kel.

On the other hand, the suits had made serious, if largely ineffective efforts, to save me. If Kel had wanted me dead, why had he assigned people to protect me?

This seemed to make Kel a good guy. Which meant there was something or someone in the mix we didn't know about. Maybe round head had seen me and it had taken him that long to track me down. He could have taken the license plate number off the car and had it traced. Or someone at the police station could have tipped him off.

I liked this scenario better than the one where Kel kissed me, then tried to get me killed. And not just because he kissed like a romance hero. He didn't feel like a bad guy to me. Sometimes a girl just had to trust her heart.

Thanks to these cogitations and despite my near death experience, I was light of heart when I made my shoeless way home and found a yummy looking white Porsche occupying my spot in front of the house.

I shut off my car and opened the door. That's when I heard the category five din emanating from Rosemary's house. In the backyard I could also hear Addison barking furiously.

When I looked at the new suits, they looked away.

My heroes.

Dog first. I found him in the backyard with Rosemary's baby. Dom was perched on the fence in full pirate regalia, brandishing his plastic hook hand.

"What's with the noise, Blackbeard?"

"Ar, Candy's on the phone," Dom growled.

"Oh. Right." Of course, that would explain the noise level, wouldn't it? "Why's Addison barking like that?"

"There's a scalawag up our tree. I'm going to give him a peg leg when he comes down."

"Really?"

With his plastic sword, he gave me one instead. I mock-limped my way round the corner to the tree Addison had staked out. It was a particularly fine cherry tree, despite being winter bare. Dom hadn't imagined it. There was a man up there.

Kelvin Kapone.

He looked particularly fine sitting up a tree.

He looked even better out of the tree. His soft dark chocolate tee shirt was tucked into khakis that fit smoothly across romance hero thighs. His brown leather jacket gave him a relaxed, rakish aura. The sunlight filtering through the bare branches of the tree found each strand of gold in his light brown hair and his blue eyes were both sheepish and amused.

"Sorry about that," I said.

He was remarkably poised for a man who'd been treed by a

dog, then given a *coup de peg leg* by a six year old pirate. Perhaps Kel recognized his own kind in Dom.

He smiled at me, the dimple came into play, igniting lust. My heart started this tom-toming in my chest. Between fear and lust, the old ticker was getting quite the workout.

"So, what were you doing up my sister's tree?"

"I came to see if you have a license for that glue gun."

Repeated exposure to his charm was giving me, if not immunity, at least the ability to be reasonably coherent while basking in it. I grinned. "You going to arrest me if I don't?"

His smile widened into wicked. "No, but I might have to search you."

"Well," I plucked a twig from his hair, "my mother taught me to be law abiding, so I guess I'd have to let you." My mother hadn't taught me to play with fire, but she probably knew that came naturally. My words put a satisfying blaze in his blues eyes.

It was like believing I was the rabbit and finding out I was really the magician.

"Never let it be said," his mouth curved dangerously, "that I didn't do my duty."

The hand he held out to me had a slight tremor in it. I felt an echoing one rattle my knees. At this rate, I wouldn't have a solid bone left in my body.

When his palm made contact with my skin, we both sighed. His fingers spread, then slid around to the back of my neck, starting fires on the way. His head bent toward my mouth. My mouth parted, eager for tutoring in the delights of the flesh.

In the background, the pounding rock'n roll kept time with my heart.

He took his time, was very thorough. As a taxpayer, I was pleased and felt entitled to some searching of my own. I spread my hands over the tee shirt and the chest underneath, felt his heart pound into my palms. Felt it pound for me. I was careful to keep my hands above the bandage, but that left plenty to be explored and enjoyed. The wonder of it spread down to my toes. I went up on them to get closer. He helped, wrapping his arms around me and deepening his search.

"Stan? What are you doing?"

Dazed, and not a little annoyed, I peered around Kel's shoulder. Joelle and Justine were staring solemnly up at us. I could have ignored them. They'd seen worse on television. But what I couldn't ignore was the stump on the left side of each small head where a braid used to be.

The noise was worse inside. Everything that could be turned on had been turned on. At the epicenter, I found Candice lying on the floor with her feet propped up on the wall, talking on the phone as if she were in the sound proof booth of a TV game show.

I unplugged the telephone, her mouth forming a protest I couldn't hear, and sent the twins off on a quest to restore quiet. Conversation was impossible until they succeeded. Candice came after me, trailing the dismembered telephone and an inaudible whine, until silence spread through the house. She caught sight of Kel leaning against the counter next to me and stared at him with cow eyes.

"Whoa, who's this?"

I performed introductions, then stood back and watched Kel give her his dimpled smile. She visibly melted. Did I look like that, I wondered. Did I care?

The twins returned from their quest for silence and promptly leaned against Kel's legs, gazing up at him with adoring expressions. Lucky little brats. Kel looked at me inquiringly and I shrugged back. Hey, children attaching themselves to your legs is just one of the many hazards of the suburbs. I turned towards another one. The teenager.

"So, where's your mother and grandmother?"

"There was this shoe sale."

I didn't need further explanation. My mother and my sister suffer from Imelda Marcos Syndrome, an incurable addiction to shoes.

"And they left you in charge of the asylum?"

She looked sulky. "Yes."

I turned Joelle's and Justice's heads so she could see the ragged stumps of hair. "Perhaps you can tell me what happened to the braids that are usually right here?"

"Ar, I like it," Dom said. Addison gave a big woof, but it was hard to tell if he approved or disapproved.

Candice, who knew she was in serious trouble, gave a high-pitched shriek that I was sure broke some glasses in the cupboard behind us. I could have pursued the inquiry, but it had all the hallmarks of a Teaching Moment. I didn't have to do those anymore.

"I guess I'd better run them through Supercuts."

"Good. We can hit the video store," Candice, of the notoriously short attention span, said.

"By all means, let me reward your irresponsible behavior." I know that sarcasm is wasted on teenagers. I just like making futile comments that fall on deaf ears. I looked uncertainly at Kel. Now that he'd checked my license to pack a glue gun, why was he still here?

"I'm game if you are." He gave the braid stumps a friendly pat. The twins visibly preened.

"You're sure you don't have to save the world or something?"

"Only from nine to five. I'm on my own time now."

I smiled clear down to my toes. If I had to go out in public with small children and teenagers it was nice to be in the care of a highly trained, professional government agent.

Since my mother and Rosemary took her van, we had to decide whether to stuff six people into my Honda or his Porsche. Naturally the kids wanted to go in the Porsche.

"It's too small," I said, not without regret. It would be great to zip along in a Porsche with a spy at the wheel.

"Simone's mother says men buy cars as phallic symbols," Candice said, chattily.

I choked back a laugh, but had to look at Kel. He grinned. "It's small, but it has plenty of power under the hood."

"What's a phallic?" Joelle asked.

It was my turn to grin. "Man's best friend."

Justine frowned. "It's a dog?"

Kel choked.

"In your dad's case it is," I said, unsteadily.

Kel told the body guards to stay put, then we all squeezed into the Porsche and took off. It was a rare privilege watching a government operative handle, with varying degrees of success, three children and a teenager. When we finally arrived back home, I had a feeling some nice, cold-blooded terrorists or some KGB agents would have looked pretty good to him.

The brood straggled into the house, leaving us standing by the Porsche. Whatever doubts I might have had about him were gone. If he was going to kill me, he would have done it during the outing and saved himself from teenage angst.

And I might have thanked him, I admitted, barely repressing a shudder at the memory of what we'd endured at Chuck E.'s Pizza. There ought to be laws against letting children congregate in packs and fuzzy, semi-animated singing creatures.

"That was interesting," Kel said. He shoved his hands into the pockets of his coat and shrugged his shoulders slightly, as if to adjust the fit. I realized I'd seen him do it before, usually when our talks turned personal. That was interesting.

It made my breath catch just looking at him. There was a warm feeling of rightness about the ordinary things I'd done with him. He'd injected something into my life I didn't want to feel. Something I didn't want to miss when the spy went back to saving the world and I went back to drawing my stupid roach.

"I'd ask you in," I said, "but it would be cruel and inhumane."

"Why?" He stepped closer, drawing his hands out of his pockets and putting them on my hips, urging me gently closer. It didn't take much urging, though I did allow myself one nervous look back at the house.

"My mother."

"Oh." There was a wealth of understanding in the single syllable.

"She wants me married with children so I'll know what she went through. Otherwise, all those years of hoping I have one just like me will be for nothing. She's probably watching us out the window right now."

His face lit with a smile that was slow and potent. "Then we ought to give her something to see."

If we gave her something to see, it would give her lots to say, but even knowing I was in for a grilling and a lecture, I didn't hold back.

I was getting used to his taste and the shape of his mouth. I was learning to read how I made him feel, to sense my own power. Heady stuff for my mother's daughter.

I ran my hands over his chest to rev his motor. He was right. There was a lot under his hood.

I was humming when he drove away. The best part? My mother wasn't watching. She was trying on shoes with Rosemary.

There is a God.

I gave thanks as I went upstairs to my room.

Chapter Fifteen

The blinking light on my answering machine had a peculiar insistence that dug through my pleasure. Reluctantly I rewound the tape and pushed play.

"Isabel, Muir here—" I punched up the next message. This one was from Reverend Hilliard, reverently informing me of the time and place for Mrs. Carter's funeral tomorrow. It appeared that Mrs. MacPhearson was still on the injured list. The last message was from the guys.

"Yo, Stanley! Jerome here. Wanted to clue you in on tonight's happening at the Rad. It's Dirty Dancing night, so wear something hot, okay? We'll be out front at ten-three-o to collect you in Drum's truck."

A truck. Three young men. And the CIA watchdogs. Sounded like the title of a movie. A disaster flick.

After almost getting killed it felt quite reasonable to don black leggings with lace at the ankles and an electric red silk top for a date with three young men. I felt, not Isabel-ish but not Stan-ish either, as I unbraided and brushed my waist length hair until it crackled like the pit of my stomach during Kel's kisses. Once the tangles were out, I piled it into a decorative wad on the crown of my head.

Perhaps this was how Rosemary felt? And why she was able to be all she could be, when she wanted to. I felt alive again, filled with an anticipation I hadn't felt since high school graduation, as if my life, and maybe even the world, was just waiting for me to jump in and experience it.

I attached dangly gold earrings from New Orleans to my lobes, traced red around my mouth and pursed. I was ready to smile, flirt, dance and get kissed.

I just hoped the guys were ready for me.

I was watching for them when they came. I didn't want them honking and alerting the neighborhood or my mother. The suits looked a bit startled when I climbed into Drum's beat-up pick-up truck. Since it wasn't a stretch cab, I sat on Tommy's lap and shifted. With each passing minute I got younger. By the time we arrived at the Radical, I was eighteen.

I swept into the Radical Club surrounded by boys. It was the kind of place you could. Surprisingly upscale with lots of neon. And lots of boys and girls. The dance floor had the obligatory glitter ball hanging over it. On all four walls, giant screens were angled for viewing music videos, though this evening they featured scenes from the movie, "Dirty Dancing." At any other time it might have been unnerving to have Patrick Swayze's hips coming at me from four different directions, but not tonight.

Tonight, I had no nerves.

In a dark corner was the bar. Against the back wall, surrounded by brilliant, white lights was the final service provided by the club: a small stage on which patrons can make the unnatural progression from spectator to drunk to lip-synch performer with the maximum attention. The whole room was bathed in a pinkish glow with tracks of red neon lighting cutting through a smoky haze that must have been artificially induced since smoking was prohibited. My suits looked as much at home as Jesse Jackson would at a Klan meeting.

I felt young, but did my hips know it? The music swept over me and my hips twitched, then went for it.

I still had it.

The flickering lights, swaying bodies and sensual sound weren't "oldies" to me but a magic carpet of sound sweeping me back to a time when I didn't just feel brand new, I was brand new.

Only this time I wasn't adorning the wall. I was with three, count 'em, three totally rad, totally virile young men.

It wasn't as fun as locking lips with Kel, but not much would be. Though their obvious delight in my company as I adapted my body to the sexy, swaying "dirty dancing" came very close. In between dances they plied me with Cokes and "hip" talk. When all that liquid moved lower and signaled a need to exit, I heeded that signal, excused myself and went hunting the ladies room.

That's when I got the first chink in my armor. The girls were children playing dress up and talking about actors and singers I'd never heard of. Their wondering eyes pierced my calm like the Storm smart bombs were piercing concrete. I kept my chin up, but suddenly felt weary. Feeling young wasn't the same as being young.

It was time to go home and collect my kiss.

I caught a wave of young things heading out the door and let them sweep me back down the narrow hall to the main room. A counter surge peeled me off that group. I swam up stream, tripped on some steps, climbed them to break free of the current. Someone grabbed me from behind and dragged me backwards up the rest of the stairs. For a moment, I hoped it was Kel. A very short moment.

"Don't be shy now, darling!" A brash voice assaulted my ears. It was the lip-synching MC and he'd mistaken me for a drunk in search of time in the spotlight.

"No!" I protested and started to struggle. This was not a spot I wished to inhabit.

"We got ourselves a live one, people!" he shouted into the mike, while somehow managing to keep a death grip on me. Someone turned the lights up to a white hot brilliance that turned the areas around the stage black. I blinked in the glare and tried to shake my head. I wasn't a live one. I was a nearly dead one.

"Let's give a Rad Welcome to the gal with Hungry Eyes!"

The crowd cheered gustily. He looked at me.

"You know the drill, honey?"

"I don't . . ."

"All you gotta do is read, sweet thing. If you can't sing, they won't remember it tomorrow. Give a big smile and show some skin if you got it. If you don't, show some anyway."

Before I could object, he gave me a pat on the butt and trotted off the stage, leaving me alone in a circle of light. Over cheers and catcalls I heard the intro for my impromptu and involuntary performance beginning somewhere outside the lights. The only way off this stage now was to sing. I squinted at the TelePrompTer, coming in as smooth as chocolate on cue. It was easy. I'd had hungry eyes since laying them on Kel.

The crowd responded noisily. With more confidence, I gave a wiggle of my hips. That launched a round of cheers. Cool. Their approval and the music wrapped around my heart like silk ribbon and soft velvet, trimmed with hearts and flowers. It seemed right to sing a love song when I was falling in lust with Kel, so I gave it all my lungs got and then some.

"That was great!" the MC interrupted my bows and shoved me towards the edge of the stage. He already had his next victim.

Hands reached up to help me down.

"Thank you!" I jumped, staggered slightly. The hands gripped painfully hard. I looked up to protest and found myself nose to nose with the round-headed man.

I opened my mouth to scream, but he covered my mouth with a meaty fist and shoved my face into a beefy, polyester shoulder. It smelled so strongly of cheap cologne and garlic that I gagged. He dragged me. I dragged my heels. It didn't stop him. A door slammed and we were outside. He gave me a shove that sent me reeling across the alley into a brick wall. I promptly slid down it into a pile of trash.

"You've made things hard, bitch. I oughta make it hard back, but I don't have no time."

Massacre the language, then me. I pushed my failed do off my face and tried to think. Run. Get him talking, do something, I screamed at myself.

He pulled a pistol from beneath his polyester jacket and pointed it at me with a rock-steady hand. He didn't look inclined to talk. Feathery snowflakes drifted down. I stared up the barrel of his gun. Only time to pray. Maybe not even that. His fat finger began to squeeze the trigger—

I braced for impact.

Round head should have.

Someone hit him with a full body tackle. They both went down. The dark muzzle of round head's gun flared, than vanished into the shadows with the two men. Something plucked against my arm before splintering into the wall behind me.

Like a distant "Ode to Joy" the wail of approaching sirens mixed with grunts, blows, and crashes. The two men rolled in garbage, moving in and out of my view. One time I saw them with their four hands locked around the gun.

The gun was pointed at me.

Then it turned towards the man on the bottom.

Kel.

His face was contorted almost beyond recognition as he fought for his life and mine. It occurred to me that I should help. My glue gun had been returned to my sister, but a two-by-four was at hand. I grabbed it and crawled toward them.

The gun was inches from Kel's straining face. I closed my eyes and swung. The wood bounced off the round-headed man's elbow. The gun went flying, discharging as it flew. I think I felt the wind of the bullet as it whizzed by my ear.

With a heave, Kel rolled on top and slammed the round head man against the pavement. Then he slugged him.

"That's for Elspeth Carter," he grunted, "and that's for Bel." Another bone crunching slug, then they rolled out of sight again, knocking over a pile of boxes and debris. More grunts and blows, then Kel staggered out into the murky light, a dark stain forming on his shirt where his wound was. He rubbed more blood from his mouth. A box sailed out of the shadows after him. He ducked, pulled his gun.

"It's over. Give it up." The round-headed man threw a garbage can, then burst from the shadows, running down the alley away from us. Kel dropped to one knee and loosed a flurry of shots after him.

"The next one's in your back." His voice was hard and unfamiliar. A police car screeched to a stop, the lights tracing across the ground in front of me.

The round-headed man paused. It looked like his hands were going up, but the cops didn't agree. Shots thudded solidly home in round head's tacky Western-cut shirt. He stiffened, then slumped to the ground.

Figures streamed past, the white "POLICE" on their jackets the only sharp detail in the murky light. Guns ready, they approached the still figure. One man knelt and pressed his fingers to his neck, then shook his head and put away his gun.

Kel stowed his weapon, his movements labored. He turned towards me.

"You all right?" His grin was crooked, his breathing labored. He held out his hands to me. My arms felt heavy, my body shaky as adrenaline faded away.

"We've got to stop meeting like this." I tried to match his light tone. I'd seen a lot of stars wheeling past my eyes the past two days, but these stars were particularly insistent. Hot pokers of pain stabbed into my shoulder. I couldn't hold back a moan.

"Bel?"

I swayed. His grip on my hands tightened. One shifted to my waist, offering support.

"Are you hurt?"

I looked at my hand. Something was wrong with it. It wouldn't do anything and it had red, warm stuff all over it.

Blood.

"You're bleeding," I muttered. My head fell back on his shoulder. His face wavered in front of me, like a pendulum.

"That's not my blood," I heard Kel say.

Dark slammed in like the death I'd expected. For a brief instant I felt the rough texture of his coat against my face. It smelled like garbage.

Chapter Sixteen

Consciousness returned in pieces, until finally a face came into focus. One I didn't recognize. In some kind of uniform.

"Who are you?"

"So, you're back with us, are you?"

No, my brain said. My mouth didn't echo it. Memory returned the way consciousness had, in bits and pieces.

"I got shot."

"Yep. And you're suffering from shock. I've got you hooked up to an IV and you should start feeling better soon."

"How is she?" I heard Kel ask.

"Why don't you ask her, she's awake."

She disappeared and Kel took her place. It was a big improvement. I waved my hand around until he grabbed it.

"How do you feel?"

"You should know," I said.

He grinned.

"You both need to take it easy," put in the EMT. "We'll be transporting you to the hospital soon."

"No!" I tried to sit up. Kel and a lack of coordination stopped me.

"Don't get all stirred up. You'll start bleeding again." He looked over his shoulder at the EMT. "I'll have to pass on the ambulance ride, doc, but Miss Stanley will be going."

Oh really? "I didn't make you go in the hospital."

"You want me to take you to the dog doc?"

"I want to go home." I shifted my arm and had to hold back a gasp of pain. "It's not bad. Really."

"Right." Kel looked at the EMT. "How bad is she?"

"Not bad, it's just a scratch, but . . ."

"There, you see? Unhook me please?"

She looked disapproving, but did as I asked.

"You can't drive—"

"I'll be taking her home." Kel jumped down from the ambulance and then helped me down. We stopped in the shadow space between the ambulance and a building. There was an illusion of privacy, of separation from the activity around the motionless body of the round headed man.

I looked up at the drifting flakes. I couldn't look at him when I admitted, "I'm here with . . . friends."

"Friends?"

I nodded.

"One of them wouldn't be called Jerome, would he?"

I looked at him then. His face was remarkably expressionless.

"How did you know?"

"He left a message on your answering machine."

It took a few moments for my mental gears to grind round to the obvious. "You . . . bugged my phone?"

"And your apartment." He didn't look the least bit repentant.

"You—I—how could you do that?" Had they heard me singing in the shower? Of course they had. This was the CIA. They could hear a gnat pass gas if they wanted to.

"We needed to monitor the inside of your apartment for your protection. You don't have to be embarrassed. We all liked your singing. Especially Wild Thing."

I covered my face. "You could've warned me."

"If I had you would've been too quiet. I'm trying to protect you, but it isn't easy. Sneaking off for a late date . . ."

"I left in the open with your guys on my tail." It occurred to me that he sounded jealous. I started to smile. "Actually, it wasn't a date."

"Not a date?" He sounded as disbelieving as he looked.

"No. It was . . . dates."

"Dates?"

"Jerome. Tommy. Drum."

"You went out with three men at once?" He gripped my shoulders. I kind of liked his look of incredulity.

I shrugged. "Yeah, I guess they're men."

"What the hell is that supposed to mean?"

I studied his tie carefully. "They're a little younger."

"How much younger?" he asked grimly.

"Does it matter? If they'd been ten or thirteen years older than me, no one would say a word. And it's not like I seduced them. They asked me. They've been reading Cosmopolitan."

I smiled at him, inviting him to share the joke. After a moment, he started to grin and the joke was on me because I was already in a weakened condition.

"If it tells a guy how to deal with a woman like you, I'm going to get me one."

I felt the change in his hands, saw it in his eyes, as he changed from clutching to caressing. I didn't mind. I needed the heat spreading through my body.

"Are we forgetting who came through whose sun roof onto whose lap? Or is that whom's lap?" My voice wobbled slightly. He slid his hands across my back. My back liked it a lot. In the spirit of cooperation, I put my good arm around his neck.

"I can't forget anything. I sure as hell can't forget . . ." his mouth brushed the edge of my mouth, ". . . this."

He was temptation wrapped in an almost irresistible

package, but I was a proper Baptist girl with a mandate from God to try.

"You're the CIA. I'll bet you know more about me than I know about myself."

His hands slid to center back. Our hips came together like it was their reason for being. Why couldn't I belong to a religion that agreed? My blood was thundering in a way that probably wasn't wise when there was a hole in my blood stream.

"I know you're susceptible to strays and that you try to do the right thing." His mouth moved over the curving skin of my cheek. "I know you sing in the shower and smile when you sleep." He turned his attention to the area around my eyes.

I closed them and gave silent thanks for his attention to detail. "See," my words came out in little gasps, "I knew you knew . . . something . . ."

I lost track of what it was I was trying to say, when his exploration moved to where my neck and shoulder met.

"I see desire in your eyes, Bel." He traced their outline, his touch torturously sweet, erotically gentle. "But it's not enough. I want to watch them change while we make . . . fax."

I don't like admitting it, but if he'd just kept kissing me, he might have got fax. Instead he gave me a choice. He put me in charge of my own seduction.

Cold air rushed between us when I stepped back. I could tell Kel wasn't thrilled with my choice. I opened my mouth to explain, but Willis and Dillon were making a beeline for us.

If there's one thing I hate in a cop, it's lousy timing.

Both men looked at me, but Dillon said to Kel, "Got an ID on the shooter. Name of Robert Howard. Drug squad is on its way to his apartment, but I'll bet money he's not a dealer."

"He could be," Willis protested.

"No." Kel came in on Dillon's side. "I don't know what

this is about, but it isn't drugs."

"He's a red neck, not a druggie," Dillon agreed impatiently. "In the same National Guard unit as the Mitchell kid. The gun he was carrying was military issue. Mitchell was assigned to the supply depot. My gut is telling me someone was dealing in stolen military supplies."

Kel nodded thoughtfully. "Pilfering has always been a problem. With all that's going on in the Gulf, be a prime time to make some money." He sighed. "Damn. This means military intelligence will want to get involved. We get anymore government agencies sniffing around this case it'll be more crowded than the Desert Storm briefings."

Now that Kel wasn't warming me, I started to shiver. My coat was inside with the guys and I'd lost blood. It wasn't that I didn't care about this stuff, well, actually I didn't care. How could I when each shiver felt like knives stabbing in my arm? "I need to go get my coat from the club. Look, my friends can run me home . . ."

Kel quickly shrugged off his coat. "You shouldn't go back inside."

"Why not? There's no danger anymore, is there?"

Willis coughed. "You haven't had a chance to see yourself, have you Miss Stanley?"

"Oh." I guess I had kind of wallowed in garbage. And blood. I let Kel help me into his unpleasantly fragrant, but nicely warm coat. I must have looked as tired as I felt, because Kel turned to the detectives.

"Can you have someone contact Miss Stanley's friends for her?"

Dillon pulled out a notebook. "Names? Descriptions?"

I looked into his darkly sardonic face and wished I was unconscious again.

"I think you know them . . . Jerome and Tommy . . ." I

faltered as his brows rose towards his hairline. ". . . and Drum."

He stared at me for a long moment, then turned abruptly and stalked towards the club. I looked at Kel and Willis.

"He's not happy, is he?"

Someone called Kel, leaving Willis behind to stare at me with brooding gaze, until I finally asked, "What?"

"I think I have you figured out and filed away, then you pop up again. Always as the victim."

I didn't know what to say, so I didn't try.

"A great, big question mark that the CIA has thrown a blanket over, so wide that a lowly cop like me can't penetrate it. Why is that, I wonder?"

I shrugged, my arm protested, making me wince. "I don't know. I'm harmless, really."

"Harmless?" He turned and looked at the body in the black bag being wheeled past us.

I looked away. "He was trying to kill me. And he did kill Mrs. Carter and Paul Mitchell. It's not my fault he's dead."

Willis shrugged. "Well, at least Bobby can't hurt you now. You should be safe."

"I certainly hope so." I sighed. "I have to play the organ for Mrs. Carter's funeral tomorrow. It'll be easier now that I know her killer has been caught."

He nodded somberly and turned to go, then hesitated. "Did you remember that sketch you promised me?"

"What? Oh, sure. I'll get it to you real soon." When I found my sketch book. If I found my sketch book. I'd have to ask Kel if he found it.

"I guess you wouldn't reconsider giving me that one with me and Dillon in it?"

I looked at him. "You recognized yourself?"

He grinned. "Sure. You're not kind, but you're good."

"Well, I guess I could give you a copy," I said, "when I get my sketchbook back."

"Back?" He looked surprised. "Did you lose it?"

"Oh, no. Just temporarily misplaced it."

"Oh, well, I'll check back with you."

I nodded. I suppose it was the murky lighting that made his eyes suddenly look so unfriendly.

The guys were both defiant and solicitous when they arrived with Drum's dad and my coat. I think they were also chagrined they'd missed the chance to play hero. They wanted to waft me home immediately, but Kel protected me from their overly enthusiastic care by implying the police weren't done with me yet and that I would be conveyed home officially.

"This is official?" I asked, as Kel settled me into his little Porsche, then expertly maneuvered the car away from my second crime scene. Or was it my third? I'd lost count.

"You could look on it as a chance to discover for yourself what's under the hood."

I was too tired to blush, so I gave him a look.

He grinned, steering the car with a slight air of bravado, and putting the car through its paces. I'd noticed him eyeing the guys biceps and had to smile. "Your dates were a tad defiant there at the end."

"Yeah, that must have been some meeting with Drum's dad. A pity about the goodnight kiss." I started a silent count. Only got to seven.

"Goodnight kiss?"

"Yeah, they thought it wouldn't be sensitive to line up on my doorstep, so I was supposed to choose which one got it. It's probably just as well. If I picked Jerome, then what would I do about his dad?"

"Why do I feel another bombshell coming?"

"Not a bombshell. A date. With his father."

"You have a date with Jerome's father?"

"For bingo and accordion polkas. It's so depressing. He'd be perfect for my mother. She loves bingo and accordion—" I straightened up and looked at Kel, stunned by my inadvertent brilliance. "Of course. Mike fell for Rosemary. Steve can fall for my mother."

"Steve." Kel gave a half laugh. "Anyone ever tell you that you're one sick puppy?"

"Pretty much everybody. I write about a roach, remember?" I sank back in my seat, covering a yawn with my unwinged hand.

"Tired?"

"Paralyzingly."

"My shoulders may not be as broad as your young men's, but I'm told they're comfortable."

By who, I wondered, too tired to ask, but not too tired to be curious. I settled against his solid warmth, felt his strength flow into me. And whatever he thought, his shoulders were every bit as broad as the boys—unless you added them all together.

"Would you tell me something?"

I blinked sleepily. "If I can." Life with my mother had taught me to be wary of committing to unknown questions.

"What was the real reason you ran out on me yesterday?"

"I was hoping you'd forgotten that." I kept my eyes closed, hoping the discussion would go away.

"It took ten years off my life."

"Then we're almost even. You took twenty off mine when you dived through the sun roof."

"That's not an answer."

"No." I tried to ignore his expectant silence, but he was

good. Almost as good as my mother. "Let's just say I got a little mixed up . . . about who was on who's side and who was doing what to whom and leave it at that, okay?"

"You thought because I was the only one you'd told about your round-headed guy that I was trying to kill you, didn't you?" He pulled his car to a stop in front of my house and looked down at me.

"Well, yes, but not just because of that." It seemed impertinent to be using his shoulder after just accusing him of trying to murder me, so I sat up. "You kept kissing me, too."

"You thought because I kissed you . . . I wanted you dead?" I could tell he tried hard not to sound incredulous.

"It seemed logical at the time."

"And what made you decide you could trust me?" He turned to face me and the small car with the big engine shrunk to the space of a heart beat.

Why, I wondered dreamily, was he the one who made my heart beat fast? My mother had paraded a brigade of men past me, in hopes of sparking this reaction in me, all to no avail. Instead, my heart had chosen to beat for a guy I knew almost nothing about. He was a spy who could take a bullet. He was a guy who could kiss a girl right out of her principles. He drove a Porsche and had a mother. Not an impressive array of facts.

Nothing to build a future on, if a girl were inclined to think along those lines, which of course I wasn't. I'd had a front row seat for the train wreck that was my sister's venture into the murky waters of matrimony. It served to confirm my instinctive belief that men and women were incompatible beings placed on earth with a longing to be together as part of a diabolical cosmic practical joke.

None of which explained why I trusted Kel. I went for the

non-answer. "How could I not trust a man in a cherry tree? It would be un-American."

Of course there was trust and trust. I knew I could trust him with my life, but my suddenly palpitating body and my vulnerability were another story altogether. I gave him a sleepy smile.

He smiled back, seduction emanating from his pores in tempting waves. His arms slid around me. His head bent. My anticipation rose to meet him. It was every bit as wonderful as I'd expected. And I was right not to trust him.

I just hope he didn't take it personally when I fell asleep.

Chapter Seventeen

I woke face down in my bed. It shouldn't have felt wrong. I often wake face down in my bed. But something was wrong. I examined the part of my anatomy I could see without moving and found the problem. Why wasn't I wearing my pajamas?

It wasn't like me to go to bed wearing a strapless bra and brief briefs. I wiggled my head in the other direction and saw the bandage on my arm. I dredged through my memory for anything that would get me from under Kel's mouth, out of my clothes and under my covers under my own steam.

None surfaced.

I could only conclude, I'd been undressed by a spy.

And now I had to go play the organ in a church.

Goody.

I got up. Started getting ready, all the while brooding on the perfidy of a certain spy. If Kel thought that undressing a semi-conscious Baptist and tucking her in bed was acceptable behavior, then he probably thought Congress should get a pay raise. If I got the chance I was going to tell him so. If I knew who his mother was, I'd tell her, too. I'm sure she'd hate him undressing me. Suddenly I could see her. Small, delicate, beautiful. All the things I wasn't. Oh yeah, she'd hate him undressing me.

This depressing realization was perfect preparation for the funeral. My mother rode with me. She wanted to give me tips on how to promote Reverend Hilliard's non-existent courtship. I'd added harassed to depressed by the time we got to the church. We were early and I ditched her to warm up. It was a major relief to settle behind the old organ in blissful solitude. My wound bothered my playing but it was a minor irritant, that soon faded when my hands slid over smooth, cool keys, picking out some mournful blues tunes that fitted my present mood. I didn't realize I wasn't alone until I heard a giggle almost at my elbow.

I looked up and found a row of childish faces staring at me. I didn't flinch, but only because they were from my Sunday school class. Show no weakness was my mantra when dealing with the wee ones. Sometimes it even worked.

"Play something happy, Miss Stanley," one of the wee folk urged.

Since depression wasn't getting me anywhere, I launched the rollicking reggae beat of "Under the Sea" from the Walt Disney's "Little Mermaid" for them.

Unselfconsciously, they began to dance and sing along, inviting me to join their exuberance. I probably shouldn't have succumbed. I ended with a flourish and looked up, my smile fading abruptly when I saw Reverend Hilliard and my mother staring at me.

It was a relief when the funeral ended. I noticed Kel at the back, sitting with an elegant looking older woman who looked just as petite and beautiful as I'd imagined. She also looked rich and disapproving. I don't think she liked the spiritual twist I added to "How Great Thou Art." Neither did my mother. Before I could escape, Reverend Hilliard cornered me.

"I was wondering, that is, your mother thought you wouldn't be adverse to accompanying me to Bible study class tomorrow evening?"

"Bible study class?"

"We can bring dates sometimes and I thought you might enjoy it." He looked like he thought I might enjoy it. I guess a minister would have to be an optimist. Was it a sin to say no to a man of the cloth? Wasn't bingo and accordion enough punishment for the sin of lusting after Kel?

"Could I get back to you? I need to check my schedule." Anybody but a pastor would have known that was an attempted brush off. He just gave me his reverent smile.

"I'll check with you after service tomorrow."

What a week I was having.

My mother passed on the graveside service in favor of ragging on me for the sins she knew about. Outside, my car was the only car left in front of the church. As we started across the parking lot, my mother suddenly stopped with an exclamation of annoyance. "I think I've dropped my gloves."

She half turned back toward the church, rooting through her purse to be sure.

I expelled a sigh of relief at the brief respite from being lectured and kept walking. The sudden acceleration of a car had me looking around. The last time this happened, an Uzi sprayed Rosemary's car. This one didn't have an Uzi, but it was coming right at me.

I kept thinking it would swerve. When it didn't, I did a running jump onto the hood of my car, barely in time to vacate the spot before the car went over it. It didn't stop, just sped away, squealed around the corner and disappeared from sight.

"Oh here they are, in my purse." My mother turned around. "Isabel! What are you doing up there? Get down before someone sees you like that!"

I brought my knees back together and smoothed down my dress. "Didn't you see that car?"

She put her hands on her hips. "What car?"

I opened my mouth, pointed down the empty street, sighed and desisted. "I'll just get down."

I was still trembling as I slid into the car. What a close call. If it had happened yesterday, if it had been a green minivan . . . but I hadn't offended any silver Datsun's that I knew of. Uneasy, but not sure why, I took my mother home and went up to my room to mope. In the doorway, I stopped, the unease sharpening to a sense of intrusion coming from the shadowy quiet of my space.

It was over, the CIA, the police, everybody said so. So why did I have this feeling I was forgetting something important?

"Stan?"

I didn't recognize Candice until I was well on the way down from the ceiling.

"Geez, you're jumpy. What's your problem?" She stuffed a cookie in her mouth.

I could have told her, but as a teenage child of divorced parents she already had enough self-esteem problems.

"What are you doing in here?" It was a violation of the strict separation of aunt and family, and she knew it.

"I was wondering if I could borrow your old typewriter. I've got a report I need to type up for school."

"It's in my closet."

I turned wearily towards the bedroom. I had a date to be tortured by bingo, followed by getting shoved around a room to accordion music. I didn't get far when Candice called from the living room. "Stan, I can't find the cord to plug it in!"

"It's in the little compartment on the back."

Like a wave it came over me. What I was forgetting. Mrs. Carter's purse. The little blue claim slip in my coat pocket.

"That's where the cord is?" Candice said. "Wow, it's like a secret hiding place. Cool."

Yes it was. It was exactly like a secret compartment in the

back of the typewriter. Mrs. Carter had been at Kenyon Business Machines the night she died, Kel had said, at a PT-PAC meeting. The repair slip was from Kenyon. Was it possible? Could she have hidden something in the compartment of her typewriter? But why would she hide anything in her own typewriter and then take it in for repair. Unless she was afraid someone would come after her at home. Which was exactly what had happened. According to the newspaper, her house had been trashed. Maybe the round headed guy had searched for whatever Mrs. Carter was trying to give Kel before coming after us. That's probably why it had taken them so long. Ironic if what they were looking for was sitting safely at Kenyon's.

My first impulse was to call Kel. Trouble was, my theory sounded pretty far fetched rattling around inside my head. To have to actually say it out loud . . .

I write about a roach, but I do have limits to how far I'll humiliate myself. The idea had serious flaws, even I could see that. There were better hiding places than the back of a typewriter. The whole idea was silly.

Except for the fact that nothing else in her purse had produced more than dead bodies.

I could go and check out the typewriter myself, for my own peace of mind. How could I enjoy bingo when I might be withholding an important piece of evidence from the CIA?

It only took me a moment to find the slip in the pocket of my coat where I'd left it. Kenyon Business Machines closed early on Saturday, so I'd have to hurry. I grabbed purse, coat and keys.

"Candy, I have to go pick up something before the store closes and I have this date coming. Could you like, stall him for me until I get back? Maybe introduce him to Grandma?" She looked inclined to resist, so I played my trump card.

"I'll make it worth your while."

"You mean?"

"Cold, hard cash."

"You got yourself a deal."

I said my thanks with only a hint of sarcasm, grabbed my coat and ran. I made it to Kenyon's in record time and pulled to a stop in front. Inside a young woman, pretending to type gave a pointed look at the clock edging toward four, before giving me a stiff smile.

"Can I help you?"

"I came to pick up a typewriter. Here's the slip." I returned her smile with a false one of my own.

She studied the slip for a long moment, obviously a real speed reader, then slowly pushed back the chair and stood up. She was tall, well endowed, and dressed to flaunt it. As I watched her swaying hips retreat, I curled my lips in disgust. One guess which Kenyon hired her.

"Isabel, darling."

Had I conjured up the pond scum with my thoughts? I wearily turned around. Hadn't I suffered enough?

"See, darling. That's twice now I've not confused you with Rosemary."

"I'm underwhelmed."

"Why didn't we meet first? I like a woman with spirit."

"The only woman you wouldn't like is one with a sexually transmitted disease. And then you'd have to think about it."

My words just bounced off his ego. "So how's the dog doc?"

"He's dating Rosemary."

"Really?"

"Yeah, she's so happy, I'll bet she'd let you have the Mercedes back—if you offered her a financial incentive." Now that it was full of bullet holes, she didn't want it.

"Thanks for the tip. I will. Is Mimsie helping you?"

Mimsie. Why was I not surprised? "Yes, and here she is now."

The heavy typewriter accentuated the sultry sway of her hips and squeezed her breasts almost out of her low cut blouse. She squinted at the slip again. "That'll be one hundred and fifty dollars and fifty-five cents, please."

I tried not to look horrified, but it wasn't easy. I wrote out a check and handed it over with a silent farewell. It would have been nice if I could have peeked inside, just to see if I was buying something besides repairs for a typewriter I didn't own. She gave me a receipt and for better or worse, it was mine. I went to grab it, Dag didn't offer to help because gallant wasn't in his programming, but before I got my hands on it, another voice halted my escape.

"Isabel?"

Flynn Kenyon. All we needed now was Muir to complete the set. I really hated playing happy former families. I turned, summoning up a stiff smile for him.

"Flynn."

He came out of the shadows of the closing store, his smile visible first. He wasn't wearing white, but he could have been.

"You're picking up Mrs. MacPhearson's typewriter?"

What? I almost said it out loud. How could this be Mrs. MacPhearson's typewriter? Had they given me the wrong one? I was tempted to tell him, but something, maybe Dag coiled next to me, stopped me.

"Is it?" I asked. "I just told Reverend Hilliard I'd pick it up for him." I felt guilty using the Reverend to perpetuate a lie.

"The numbers on the slip matched," Mimsie whined.

"If she wants her typewriter, she must be feeling better." His face was expressionless.

"I hope so. I've been covering for her at the organ." I hooked my hands round the handle and started to lift.

"Perhaps I should check it before you go. We want everything to be in order for her, since she's not quite up to par." His tall, thin figure loomed over me, almost sinister as his hands reached for the typewriter.

"Check it?"

"That's right. It'll only take a moment to open it up." He paused, seemed to home in on my fear. "Unless you have some reason why you don't want me checking it?"

Chapter Eighteen

"Reason? I don't think so." My mind limped this way and that, looking for an out. "I was just surprised. I thought you checked everything before you brought it out. If you don't think this typewriter was properly fixed, then by all means check it."

I felt I'd lobbed his serve quite neatly back into his own court and allowed myself a small smile.

"I did check it before I brought it out, Mr. Kenyon," Mimsie plaintively asserted.

Which probably meant I'd just bought a pig in a poke.

Flynn smiled. "Then I'm sure everything is in order."

I grabbed the typewriter and staggered out the door. After slinging it into the passenger seat, I scrambled behind the wheel and squealed away from the curb. At the first light I dug at the latch of the little door. It fell open and a sheaf of papers fell out.

Computer sheets with diagrams of several buildings, boxes of figures next to each one? Not exactly the "blinding light of discovery" clue I was expecting, but certainly something that shouldn't have been in a typewriter that apparently belonged to Mrs. M.

Someone honked behind me and I tossed the sheets down, accelerated, then braked to make the turn onto the freeway ramp. I sped up again, then made the mistake of switching to that same auto pilot that had landed me in the middle of a shoot out. The straight stretch of highway made it easy to worry at the problem of what I'd got hold of. What was Mrs. Carter doing with the claim slip for Mrs. M's typewriter? And what were the diagrams? Something about them buzzed at the edge of my mind. I stole a quick peek and realized that over each diagram someone had drawn circles, small in the center, then gradually widening.

Like a target.

Traffic was flowing smoothly, so I took another quick look. The buildings weren't identified, though there was something sort of governmental about them. Anybody watching the war on television knew all about smart bombs and heat-guided missiles. Security measures had been stepped up at the airports and it was common knowledge there were Patriot missiles guarding government buildings because of the threat of terrorism.

I wasn't great at math, but I could put two and two together and get an ominous four.

A car ahead of me suddenly swerved into my lane, startling me out of my sleuth-like musings. I braked hard. The rear of my car slued in a half circle. The horizon blurred to rainbow hues as it went past. I missed the braking Datsun by inches. A Ford by millimeters. The guard rail by less than that.

No one was more surprised than I was when I found myself unharmed, heading straight and true down the road again. In my rear view mirror, I saw the Datsun swerve off an exit. Idiot, I thought, pressing down on the gas. I couldn't wait to show Kel his clue. If he was nice, I wouldn't even gloat.

Yeah, I would. I'd earned the right.

By the time I got home, my date was my mother's date, which shows that life can't ever be all bad. I don't think either of them noticed when I slipped away to call Kel about my find. I was reaching for the telephone when something moved just right of my peripheral vision.

Since everyone I knew, including my dog, was downstairs, I opened my mouth to expostulate loudly. Nothing got out because someone grabbed me and covered my mouth with their hand. I struggled madly. I was tired of getting grabbed. We staggered and reeled a bit, then tumbled onto the couch. Before we landed my senses had nailed him as friendly and I'd quit struggling.

I gave him a severe look from my spot on the bottom. "I wish you wouldn't do that."

"You surprised me," Kel said.

"I guess coming home is a nasty habit. I'm trying to stop, but until I find somewhere that isn't my home . . ."

He chose the quickest way to shut me up. It was a good choice. I wasn't going to have fax with him, but I sure liked kissing him on the mouth. And beside his mouth. And along his cheek. . . .

When we came up for air, I asked severely, "How did you get in?"

"I picked your lock. After making sure your dog wasn't here."

"Knocking is hard on the knuckles."

"And they belong to my country," he pointed out. "I'm not allowed to bang them against just anything."

There was that sense of humor again. If he didn't stop coming around I'd start believing Congress was spending too little and that love could last. And if I wasn't careful I was going to get romance writing fantasy mixed up with my reality. Not good.

I quit stroking the strong column of his neck. A girl who'd recently been to church and almost been killed several times this week, should be resisting temptation, not offering blatant invitations to the author of it.

I realized "temptation's" heart was beating as hard as mine and asked huskily, "Did you have a reason for breaking and entering or were you just polishing up your skills?"

His grin turned wry. "Actually I did."

He slid off and helped me upright. I needed the help. Our tussle had not only turned my body rubbery, it made my arm hurt.

"I need a favor."

"Okay?" I had a feeling it wasn't fax he was requesting, but I tried to look attentive and alert.

"It seems that Dillon was right on about the connection between Howard, your round-headed man, and the Mitchell kid. There's been some major pilfering going on in their guard unit. And either Mitchell and Howard had a falling out, or Mitchell found out about it and got killed to silence him. I suspect the latter, he had a clean record and Howard didn't."

"How awful." I shivered and Kel put his arm around my shoulders. I warmed myself against the furnace of his body. It was a government sponsored perk I'd helped pay for.

"It's a royal mess. Right now they're trying to find out what's missing, but with half the unit on its way to the Gulf it's not going to be easy. Howard made sure the records were all screwed up. A lot of dangerous armament could be missing and in the hands of our enemies."

"Wow." I thought about the weaponry I'd seen on CNN the past few weeks. It was scary to think of it in our hands, let alone the bad guys. "How did I get mixed up in stuff like this, Kel?"

"You drove into it. What I'd like to know is where Mrs. Carter fits in? There has to be a connection between her and the others besides PT-PAC or the drug angle."

I didn't have a clue how or where a retired schoolteacher

fit into a puzzle made up of round-headed crooks and missing smart bombs. Luckily Kel's question appeared to be of the rhetorical variety. Almost absently he stroked my hair, a slight frown pulling down his brows and a distant look in his eyes.

"If only I knew what she was trying to tell me the night she was killed. You were right about her purse. Other than the matchbook, there wasn't anything worth killing her for."

"Oh! But there was!" I gave him an apologetic look. "It fell out when I was looking at it. I put it in my coat pocket meaning to give it to you and then forgot. It didn't seem that important. It was just a repair claim ticket for a typewriter."

His look of hope faded. "Oh."

"No, I think it was the clue! I had this sort of idea, so I went and picked it up myself just now."

Hope looked good dawning in his face once more. "And?"

"Over there on the floor. I found stuff where the cord is usually stored. When you take them in, they make you keep your cord so they don't lose it, you know."

He abandoned me with a bump. I didn't mind. Really. I mean, this was national security. I wasn't even a national treasure. So I was cold without the spy hugging me. My country would be a safer place because of it. Probably.

He gathered the sheets I'd dropped when he grabbed me and started studying them with an intensity that said more than words how serious the situation was.

He looked up.

"Where was the typewriter?"

"At Kenyon Business Machines."

"Really." I could tell that interested him, but he didn't tell me why. Very close-mouthed these spies. Of course, I was only a helpful citizen and not the press, so why should he tell me anything? "Didn't you say you had a fax machine?"

I knew exactly which fax he was interested in. I pointed to my desk.

"I'd like to get my people working on this right now. There's a clock ticking in my head. I can feel it. Time is running out on this one, Bel. Fast."

"My fax is your fax, if you promise the CIA will reimburse me the money I paid for the typewriter?"

He grinned. "Our money is your money."

Truer words were never spoken. Or more ignored by the guardians of it. "Help yourself."

I figured he needed a little privacy, so I slipped into the kitchen and rounded us up something to drink. My arm was still throbbing from our wrestling match, so I tossed down a couple of aspirins before I rejoined him.

"Thanks. Do you mind if I hang around for a bit? They want to send me something in a few minutes."

He might as well have asked me if I wanted to keep breathing. I handed him the drink with a hand surprisingly steady, considering it had just hit me that I'd like him to hang around forever. I sank down on the couch, my thoughts spinning in a dazed way. How had this happened?

Pride. That was my downfall. I'd been so proud of staying heart whole, so proud that I didn't need a man in my life for contentment.

So fate had set out to humble me, to teach me about need and unfulfilled desire, about how to want what you can't have.

Kel sat down next to me, his arm sliding behind my head with a casual air that nine out of ten teenage boys would have given their virginity to emulate. There was a short silence. Now that we were no longer discussing murder and mayhem, I couldn't look at him. What if he looked in my eyes and saw a longing for more than fax between us?

"I enjoyed your playing at the funeral," Kel murmured, his husky voice turning lazy as he temporarily stood down as a spy. "Where'd you learn to jazz it up like that?"

"New Orleans." His fingers moved in my hair, taking apart my braid and setting the strands free.

"You have wonderful hair."

"Thank you." I sounded so stilted, I wanted to die.

"Is something wrong?"

"No . . . no."

He leaned closer, amusement filtering into his voice. "You don't still think I'm trying to kill you, do you?"

"No, I'm fine, really." I'm afraid you're trying to break my heart is what I wanted to say.

"You're wound pretty tight." He began to knead the back of my neck, his touch strong, but gentle.

It felt really good. It also started a different kind of tension at a different place in my body. "Maybe you shouldn't . . . I mean, well we kind of skipped a few preliminaries in our . . ."

What was it that wasn't happening here?

". . . association. I guess I'm just not used to it."

His hand was warm against the back of my neck. So naturally I shivered. Or it could have been a shudder.

"Would you believe me if I told you this isn't normal for me either?" he asked.

I didn't hesitate. "No."

He chuckled. We were so close together I felt it as a small, but very pleasant earthquake.

"Ian Fleming has a lot to answer for."

"So, you're saying you're not Bond, James Bond with a babe in every exotic city and a Porsche that can fly?"

"Exotic city babes carry disease and my car doesn't have that much under the hood."

"So I just imagined that whole bed-Pavlov-dog-scene

when you were under the influence of Mike's doggie drugs?"

His eyes lit the way they had that night, only without the foggy part. His mouth smiled the way it had that night.

My bones started to melt the way they had that night.

"I thought you said nothing happened while I was under?" he murmured, huskily into my ear.

My ear tingled, my body quivered.

"That's right." I swallowed dryly.

Embarrassment and desire don't mix very well. He had me blocked in. I couldn't disappear. So I closed my eyes. Big mistake. Gave him a clear field to make his move. He found my mouth easily. He'd been there before. I knew this, even as I let him draw me deeper into his terrifying, safe embrace.

It was like being in the eye of a hurricane, a place where I could experience the wild wonder of him without the danger.

Danger was out there, I just wasn't in it. Yet.

Passive at first, I let him explore my mouth with his, shivered when his hands spread across my back. Then, made brave by the thick honey of desire in my blood, I launched my own quest for knowledge.

It was necessary for my survival. If I hadn't thrust my hands into the springy softness of his hair, they would have flailed about aimlessly.

I kept my lips from idleness by tasting the skin at his temple. He was checking out my jaw line, so our explorations aided each other. Thought and feeling disconnected when I tasted and found him good. Like Baby Bear's porridge, like Eve's apple.

My hands fanned out on his chest, absorbing the heady sweetness of silk over flesh and blood, both warmed by a strongly beating heart. He recaptured my mouth and I sighed my thanks. And learned the eye of a man's passion isn't endless.

He matched my sigh, raised it a groan. Then took us out of the eye right into the storm. His mouth, his hands drove me back against the couch, tasting, touching, taking my passion and multiplying it so that I got back more in the exchange.

No wonder no one wanted the secret to get out on just how delightful the delights of the flesh really are.

All of the elements of a rampaging addiction were built right into my body, unleashed by his. I was on the fast track to biting the big one. You can imagine my surprise when I muttered, "I don't—" when I obviously was.

He paused. "Ever?"

"Well, not," I swallowed hoping to ease my dry throat, "yet."

"I thought girls like you were an endangered species?"

Sanity was slow to return, but remarks like that helped. "It's guys like you that made us that way."

He laughed, his strong warm hand settling against my throat to register the give away pace of my pulse. "Why? You seem to have all the right instincts."

"Yeah," I admitted reluctantly. "I noticed." It was hard to put into words what I was feeling. "I don't know you," I finally said, even thought it wasn't quite right. I did know Kel, I just didn't *know* him.

"We already know what's important."

"And that is?"

"That we want each other."

He wanted me. No, not me. My body. The fact that my body had a heart didn't matter. Not when passion was running the show.

"Does it bother you that you want me?" he asked, huskily against my mouth.

Instead of answering this loaded question, I said, "Maybe I should go to Bible Study with Reverend Hilliard."

"Reverend Hilliard?" He looked resigned. "Not another one?"

"It's not my fault."

The telephone rang, which was good because I had no idea how to explain the minister to the spy. It's at this point I realized we were on the floor. I didn't remember getting there.

My clothing was askew. So was his. Didn't remember that either. At least I still had my bra on.

"You're dangerous," he said, before scrambling up to answer the telephone. I just hoped it really was for him or I'd have some explaining to do.

Reality began to inject cold sobriety into all the places Kel had so nicely warmed. I tucked my hands behind my disarranged hair. Though he was advancing my knowledge of anatomy and human response, and hopefully making romance writing possible for me, he was doing some serious damage to my principles.

Not only had I unbuttoned his shirt, but I'd also started on his belt. If that telephone hadn't rang right then, would I have unzipped his pants? Would he have let me? And then what? Would I have let him take my theoretical knowledge into an actual experience field test?

I wasn't sure I wanted to know the answer to any of these questions. I was already way behind in my repenting. I got my Gumby limbs coordinated long enough to crawl up on the couch.

Kel came back and told me he had to go. He looked sorry. I felt relief. He didn't kiss me. We both knew what happens when you put a match to dry tinder.

With the object of my passion gone, my arm started to hurt again. Rosemary called me down to supper. I went reluctantly. My stomach felt queasy and my legs weren't steady.

Downstairs both my former dates were digging into my mother's lasagna with revolting enthusiasm. Had this really been my favorite dish? I must have been out of my mind.

"Here's your plate," my mother said, her eyes on Steve.

The room was airless and pain beat in my arm like ocean surf against a rocky beach. My collar felt tight and hot. My hands shook when I served myself. I almost dropped the plate when I sank into a chair, staring down at lasagna revolving in a slow circle.

"Isabel?" My mother's body wavered in front of me. I rubbed my forehead, my hand slipping wetly across clammy skin. She frowned. "Why are you smearing tomato sauce on your face?"

I tried to focus. "What?"

"That's not tomato sauce." Mike sounded grim and at least an ocean away. Darkness narrowed my view in a rush. My head, strangely weighted, fell forward. I saw the pasta coming at me and managed to turn my head to one side just in time.

The pop of my ear filling with pasta exactly coincided with the total dark.

Chapter Nineteen

Sunday morning I lay alone in my relatively virginal bed, staring at the ceiling and reflecting on life's little ironies. How was it that I, wounded and smeared with lasagna, bandaged by a veterinarian who preferred my sister, assisted by the veteran who preferred my mother—how was it that I was the one in the dog house?

Okay, I should have mentioned to my mother about getting shot. Was that grounds for ostracism? Rebellion raged in my soul as I dressed for church, moving as stiffly as an old woman. Had I recently felt young? Oh hubris!

Grimly I collected my purse, eased on a coat, and flying the flags of defiance, I let myself out through the garage so no one could see me in time to ignore me. Perhaps Reverend Hilliard would be inspired to speak on repentance or compassion. The guilt definitely needed to be spread around this house a little.

My car was parked at the curb, where I'd left it yesterday in my hurry to contact the CIA. I inserted my key, then pulled open the door. As I stepped off the curb and bent to get in, the front door opened.

"Stan!" What, was someone actually speaking to me?

"I have choir practice, Rose. I'm almost late."

"You're wanted on the phone."

I hesitated, then tossed my purse on the seat, closed the door and started to backtrack. "Do you know who it is?"

"I'm not sure. I think it's . . ."

What she thought was lost when the world exploded behind me. Heat licked at my back. The sidewalk curled up, then slammed me in the face.

I opened my eyes to semi-darkness, the silence broken by a steady beep-beep somewhere off to my right. I felt a little fuzzy around the edges, but not so much that I couldn't deduce I was in a hospital and someone was gently rubbing my hand. I turned towards the touch.

"Bel?" The dark figure moved closer and became Kel. Without waiting for instructions from my scrambled brain, my lips smiled faintly.

"We've got . . . to stop . . . meeting like this." The smile that brightened his face was almost too much for my weakened condition. "What happened?"

"Someone planted a bomb in your car. Delayed timer. Opening the door activated the device, shutting it triggered the timer."

"Oh." Trust the CIA to tell you more than you wanted to know.

"You were damn lucky, Bel. It was designed so that most of the explosive force was directed up, or you still might have been killed."

"Well, that's a happy thought." I shivered. "What I don't get is, why? It's over. You all said it was over."

"We thought it was. Or I wouldn't have pulled off the tail."

"I'm not blaming you. I just want to know who wants me dead that bad . . ." I couldn't go on.

"Did you tell anybody about the computer sheets?"

I frowned, trying to think, not an easy task with bomb echoes still reverberating through my cranium.

"No, no one knew but you."

Kel stood up, restlessly pacing, his hand kneading the back of his neck. My hand felt bereft and cold.

I frowned. "I drove that car yesterday. It didn't blow up."

"The bomb had to have been planted last night."

Into my scrambled brain filtered the memory of my two, Datsun-related near misses. "I wonder . . ."

"What? If you know something Bel, you have to tell me, even if it implicates someone you trust."

"It's nothing like that. It's just that, well, yesterday there were a couple of tiny accidents that could have killed me."

Kel's face hardened to grim. "What happened?"

I told him about the parking lot at church and the freeway near miss. He frowned.

"I can see why you weren't sure. Could have been accidents—if it weren't for the bomb."

I didn't want to think about the bomb, so I asked, "Did you find out what those papers I found meant?"

Kel stalked to the window, then back to my bed, a caged frustration to his movements that really brightened the drab room. He looked at me for a moment, then sighed. "I don't suppose it can hurt to tell you they're computer models of embassies in the DC area."

"Embassies? That's bad."

"It's not good. Particularly since we've been expecting the Israelis and the Egyptians to be terrorist targets. Now we need to find out how and when."

For the first time I noticed how tired and drawn he looked. I wasn't his only worry. "I'm sorry. I wish I could help you."

He looked at me somberly. "Someone thinks you can help us. Or they wouldn't be trying to kill you."

"But I can't. I don't know anything." It was practically the theme of my existence.

"You may not know what it is that you know." He sat on the edge of the bed and clasped my hands comfortingly. "It could be something that doesn't even seem part of this, something that seems innocent."

"If I don't know what it is that I don't know, then how can I tell you what it is that someone thinks I know before they kill me?"

My head spun with the effort of putting that sentence together. Which made me think of the pasta. I closed my eyes.

"Well, try not to worry about it." Kel stroked the hair back from my face. I focused on sensation, firmly rejecting any attempt to conjure up a picture of what I must look like after nearly being blown up. "You just concentrate on getting well. If you can relax, maybe you'll remember what it is."

"How can I remember what I don't know?" I muttered, wondering about a villain that would so completely over estimate my capabilities. It couldn't be someone who knew me very well. "If they hadn't tried to blow me to pieces I'd write these bad guys off as buffoons."

Kel looked suddenly thoughtful, as if I'd said something useful. "There does seem to be a certain lack of cohesion to this whole enterprise. I wonder . . ."

"What?"

"I've been trying to make all the pieces fit into one, big pattern. But what if it's not one pattern? What if it's several smaller patterns, each with it's own agenda, with only the final objective unifying them?"

Wow, what a torturously devious mind he had.

"You ever been taken in a shell game?"

I frowned and wished I hadn't. "No?"

"The thing about a shell game is, what you see isn't the important part. It's what you don't see that matters."

Then again, he could be cracking under the strain. I knew

I was cracking under the strain.

He stood up. "I got some things to check out."

"You're leaving?" I stared at him in alarm.

"Just for a bit."

"You can't leave me here, in a hospital." I tried to sit up.

He tried not to smile. "Why not?"

"It's not safe!"

"There's a guard posted outside the door."

"Oh, right. Like that's going to help. Why don't you just shoot me yourself and get it over with. It would be more merciful."

"Bel, you shouldn't get agitated—"

"When you were unconscious and helpless did I take you to a hospital?" Let him answer that, if he could.

"You took me to a vet who gave me dog painkiller. Is that what you want?"

"What I want, is to walk out of here on my own two feet. Not be carried out feet first in a black bag." I flung back the covers but got tangled in the paraphenalia I was hooked to.

Kel pushed me gently back in the bed.

"Oh, no you don't."

I became aware of the intimacy of our position. Faces close together, panting breaths and tangled limbs, the only thing left was for our mouths to meet.

I'm not sure which of us jumped higher when the door suddenly popped open. Or who looked more surprised. Me, Kel, or the two nurses in the doorway.

"Your heart rate shot up so suddenly . . ." one of the nurses said. The other was too busy looking at Kel.

My color shot up, too. I took my hands off Kel's shoulders so he could get off my bed. "I'm doing just fine. In fact, I want to go home."

"The doctor will be in to check you soon, Miss Stanley,"

one nurse said, soothingly, like I was a little kid. "Until then, try to stay calm, or we'll have to sedate you."

"Oh great, make it easier to kill me."

Instead of helping me, they swished out again, but not before they gave Kel a sympathetic look. Kel grinned.

"Traitor. Before you abandon me to execution, could you get me some paper and a pencil?"

"Is it a good idea to draw scurrilous pictures of people who can sedate you?"

"I'm not going to draw pictures," I informed him, haughtily, "I'm going to write my Will."

"Bel," he sighed heavily, "you're as safe in this room as . . . as—"

"As my money in an S&L? My tax dollars with Congress?"

"Nothing is going to happen to you in this hospital."

"Great," I fell back with my arms crossed, "what little chance I had is gone."

"What?" He shook his head.

I hated to do it, because I don't like to use clichés, but he deserved it. *"Famous, last words."*

He kissed my forehead. "I'll come back when you're calm."

At least I'd confirmed what I'd always known. There's no such thing as a perfect man.

Chapter Twenty

A hospital is *not* the place you want to be if someone's out to kill you. I felt like a target had been hung around my neck. Like I had a "kick me" sign on my back that said "shoot me." How could the "spy who lusted after me" not see that? How could he leave me here unprotected and alone?

Only I wasn't alone. I could feel it. I looked up. A dark figure stood in the doorway to my bathroom. I let out a squeak that tried, and failed, to be a scream.

"Are you, like, all right?" The threatening figure hurried over to me, dissolving into a cute little candy striper.

"Yeah, sure." It was probably good for my heart to leap into my throat and beat wildly. A good thing I wasn't hooked up to the monitors anymore or an alarm would have gone off. With all the years I'd lost off my life this week, I should have died last year.

I made sure my gown was tucked securely around my bare butt, then looked her over.

Blonde hair, vacant blue-eyes and a stripe-crossed bust-line of near Akasma proportion. The air escaping from her brain ruffled my hospital and bomb hashed hair. My pity wallow had been disturbed by a walking, talking cliché.

And Kel thought this wasn't a dangerous place. Ha.

"How did you get in here?"

"There's like, well, this other door in your bathroom and they aren't guarding it, so I just, like, came in."

"Really." A candy striper, slash bimbo, had beaten the CIA's security system. How comforting. "Why?"

"Some of your friends," she blushed deeply, an indication which friends, "asked me to tell you they came to visit, but the police, like, won't let anyone in."

That explained my isolation. Not content with leaving me at the mercy of killers, Kel had made sure I wouldn't have my young men to comfort me while he was off saving the world from terrorism. I had to suspect his motives for banning their visit.

"I would've liked to see them."

"They're like, downstairs in the lounge." She smiled vacantly. "They thought maybe you could, like, come down?"

I smiled evilly. "Like, I think I will."

We stuffed a bunch of pillows under my blanket, dimmed the lights, and slipped quietly out through the bathroom. My guard was reading a magazine and didn't notice me. He did pause to leer at the candy striper.

I found the dreary lounge brightened by a banner that read, "Get Weel, Stanley!"

Good thing I wasn't interested in their brains.

They were huddled over a table with their backs toward the door.

The intro to "Wild Thing" began to pulse out of the Karaoke machine they'd brought. Tommy turned, a microphone in his hand and flashed me with his smile.

It was just what the doctor hadn't ordered.

When they started singing and shaking their young booty, more than my heart was singing. Let me tell you, bumping and grinding with three buff young things is a great way to get rid of a headache.

"This is crazy." It didn't matter that I was dressed in a

puke colored hospital gown or that the patients and guests scattered around the room were pointing and staring. It didn't matter that my mother would be pissed or that someone was trying to kill me.

I'll be the first to admit it probably wasn't smart of me to party hearty so soon after being nearly blown up. But hey, if the soul doesn't survive, then what good is a working body?

I let the music and the guys' hungry looks wash over me, shimmying and swaying, lapping up soul food like an Israelite going after that first manna.

Jerome twirled me around, then pulled me against his virile chest and whispered in my ear, "So, Stanley, we gonna tie it?"

Our hips moved together as neatly as Swayze and Gray. Maybe it was my near death experience that made everything, so real, so intense I could have drawn the texture of his skin and each movement of his mouth with my eyes closed.

"Tie what?" I slid my hands down his arms and arched back, Jerome supported my weight and spun us around, then brought me back up again.

"The knot. You know, the big M. Marriage. You'd be, like, great for me, you know."

This wasn't real. It couldn't be, so I smiled and dropped, my legs sliding between his. "How can I marry you when you look better in shorts than I do?"

He laughed, pulled me up and back into his arms and put his cheek against mine. It was smooth, like a baby's butt.

"If I promise never to wear shorts, will you say yes?"

He was beautiful and he looked like he really meant it. This was a different kind of temptation from what I'd felt with Kel. That was desire. Lust. Passion. Maybe the promise of love. Or a one night stand.

Jerome's admiration tempted my ego, whispered a

promise of getting my past back, only better this time. He could wipe away the slings and arrows of adolescence with a single smile. He'd keep me young longer (though I'd probably age faster when I did) and be the perfect thing to take to my high school graduation.

It was probably a good thing the SWAT team burst through the door like a horde of commandos on speed and trained multiple weapons on us.

Who knows what I might have said in my weakened condition?

Less than a week ago, I thought the worst thing in my life was making a spit rainbow with Freddie Frinker. Since then I'd been shot at, chased, nearly blown up, woke up with a man, been covered with bras and panties in front of him, tripped over a body and had my first proposal interrupted by the SWAT team and my mother.

It was obviously time for me to reclassify "worst."

"Did you have to frisk that old man?" I asked Willis, the only person besides the SWAT team who wasn't looking daggers at me. "It's pretty obvious he's unarmed and has been for sometime."

Willis ignored me, so I looked at the guys. They were spread-eagle against the wall being carefully, and unnecessarily, frisked under the stormy gaze of Detective Dillon. Like they could be hiding a gun in those tight jeans.

"Isabel!"

I flinched, jerking my gaze off their butts and on to my mother. It wasn't near as much fun.

"Stop that!"

"I was almost blown up today. Couldn't you cut me a little slack?" Of course she couldn't. Behind her I saw Jerome and Drum each turn to face an irate father. My mother's standard, "What is wrong with you?" diatribe rained down on my again aching head. She finished with, "Look at poor Steve!"

I looked. He did have a peculiar look on his face. Maybe he'd found out his son wanted to marry me and his double standard was bothering him.

"I think you've lost your mind." She abruptly abandoned me for Steve, who had sunk into a chair and covered his face with his hands.

I'd like to think he was hiding his shame, but he probably didn't have any.

All around me the storms of discord raged. I realized that somehow I'd landed in the peaceful eye. Though multiple ire was directed at me, attention was pointed elsewhere. A shift in SWAT movement suddenly left me a clear path to the door. Of course I took it. It was safer than staying. The people who wanted me dead right now were all in that room.

At least, that's what I thought until I got back to my room. While I was dirty dancing with the boys, someone had killed my pillows.

I was sitting in a chair staring at the feathery carnage when Kel burst in with his gun out. He stopped abruptly when he saw me sitting in the chair by the bed.

I gave him an accusing look. "I told you I wasn't safe in here."

"You're damn well not safe anywhere!" His face was white, lines cut deep on either side of his mouth. Not a dimple in sight. Nor expected any time soon.

"You're angry with me?"

"I got here fifteen minutes ago. The guard was missing. And I found—" He gestured toward the bed.

"Pillows."

He gritted his teeth, ground out between clenched lips.

"I didn't know that at first."

"Okay. But now, shouldn't you be, well, relieved?"

"I've just spent the last half hour trying to find you. Why can't you stay put instead of wandering off with your . . ." He ground his even, white teeth ruinously together.

I crossed my arms. "If I'd stayed put I'd be dead instead of those pillows. Are you angry I *didn't* get killed?"

"Of course not." He didn't say it with near enough conviction. "I just wish I could understand what you . . ." He shoved his hands through his hair. "What the hell were you doing?"

"Dancing. Most cultures don't consider that a hostile act and call in a SWAT team."

"I'm supposed to be protecting you, damn it! This isn't the dating game!" He paced away from me, his hands clenching and unclenching.

Even pissed off he looked real good.

"Would you be this angry if you'd caught me dancing with some guys my own age?"

"Dancing is not the issue! Your safety is!"

"I was safer with them than I was here! A candy striper breached your precious security!" I jumped up and met him on his return pace. His nostrils flared, but I didn't back down.

"I don't know what you see in them anyway!"

I gave an incredulous half laugh. "You've got to be kidding."

His face went white as he fought for control. It did rather nice things to his chest and arms, which pissed *me* off.

"Do you think its ethical to encourage them like that?"

"They don't need much encouragement." I turned away. "And they're very nice young men."

"Nice? What are they doing chasing after a woman old enough—"

I spun around. "If you say I'm old enough to be their mother, I'll pop you! I'll have you know their attentions are strictly honorable. Jerome wants to marry me!"

I didn't want to see his surprise, so I sat on the edge of the bed and shoved a finger through one of the bullet holes in my blanket. A whiff of gun powder smell drifted up past my nostrils, briefly replacing Kel's after shave scent. The silence went on so long, I finally caved.

Kel had a weird look in his eyes. "You're not seriously considering that boy's proposal?"

I picked up a pillow and pulled some feathers out, letting them drift to the floor. "Why not? Statistically women live longer than men, which means we'd be together longer." His gaze narrowed dangerously. I narrowed mine back. "Besides, I like the irony of it. My mother's been after me since puberty to get married. She's thrown every man she could beg, bribe, or blackmail into my lap. I've suffered through blind dates with geeks, goons, and globs of humanity who all had one thing in common. Their overwhelming belief they were god's gift to women and I was lucky to have a brief moment of their time."

I threw the pillow aside and stood up.

"And now I have this wonderful opportunity, this chance of a lifetime. A guy who thinks he's lucky to be with me! And he's the one guy in the world my mother wouldn't want me to marry! Give me one good reason why I shouldn't say when and where to that boy?"

He pushed his hands through his hair. Turned away, then back. "You're out of your mind."

"Now you sound like my mother."

I think he knew I didn't mean it as a compliment.

We glared at each other across the drift of feathers.

"Really."

Something in the way he said that single word sent a cold chill down my spine. Before the thought fully formed, he was in front of me, radiating danger. His gaze had a Rhett Butler overtone when he got a lock on mine. My brain was saying, "Run, you fool!" My body just stood there and let him grip my hips and jerk me against his chest. I ordered it not to, but my head ignored me and fell back.

My mouth said, "Let me go."

"When I'm sure you know the difference between a man and a boy, I will."

I thought he was going to strangle me, but he kissed me. It wasn't a gift. No gentle wooing of lips and heart. No slow invitation to dance in passion's storm with a lover. The sound and fury of a man with a point to make pounded my defenseless lips like a wild storm against a vulnerable shore. The worst part was, I responded. Even when his mouth taunted me with might-have-beens, took without giving back.

He let me go so suddenly I stumbled back onto the bed. My mouth throbbed. And still wanted more. Stupid mouth. I rubbed it with a hand that trembled.

"And you would be the . . . what?" I looked at him, accusation stabbing from my eyes. It got him in the ego. His own idealism did the rest of it for me.

"Damn it, Bel, I'm sor—"

The door opened abruptly. Kel reached for his gun, stopping the movement when he saw my mother.

"Isabel?" Her brows rose when she saw Kel. "Who are you?"

With clipped voice, Kel introduced himself as one of the men working on the case. He looked at me, hesitated, then said, "I have to go."

At the door he turned. "They'll be moving you to another room." He nodded toward the night stand. "I brought your sketch pad. One of my men found it in the limo. You won't want to forget it again."

"Thank you." I couldn't look at him. Not with my mother watching. Not now when I was reeling from the feelings he'd aroused. This man had something I'd vowed no man would ever have: the power to hurt me. That scared me more than the person that wanted to kill me.

I looked down at my hands until the swish of door marked his leaving. I was alone with my mother. I heard her walk my way. She sat down beside me and put her arm around me.

"You all right?"

I leaned against her and quit trying to hold back the tears. "I wish I was dead."

I felt her stroke my hair. "It'll be better tomorrow."

I didn't believe her, but it was nice to hear.

Chapter Twenty-one

I had no intention of feeling better in the morning, but I'm lousy at pathos. I tried watching television, but even the war couldn't hold my attention and the mystery Rosemary had brought me to read was far less amazing than the real one I was involved in.

There was only one thing I could do when my brain was running like a mouse in the maze. I grabbed my sketch pad, intent on venting my spleen by sketching everyone who came in. And I didn't intend to be even slightly flattering.

Unless it was someone with a needle.

I flipped slowly through the pages, looking for a clean start, and came across the sketch I'd promised to the good cop, Willis. I'd made a good job of it on both of them. Dillon's bad cop glared out me from under the fur hat. His crossed arms contrasted nicely with his dancing feet. Willis fish-eyed surprise wasn't kind, but it was funny. I loved it when good sketch came together—

My thoughts splintered when I saw the tiny sketch in the corner.

The round-headed man?

When had I added him to the mix? Had to be right after I drew the two cops. The page had been clean when I started. I gave a tiny shudder. There was nothing to like in the caricature of a dead man.

"You need to watch the doodling without thinking, girl," I

muttered. It had gotten me in trouble in school and had almost gotten me killed. If I hadn't drawn it, the round-headed man wouldn't have come after me—

Wait a minute. How had he known about the sketch?

I didn't even know about the sketch. Not consciously. I frowned, my thoughts reluctantly returning to my subterranean encounter with round head. No, I didn't imagine it. He said something about me drawing him when he demanded my purse. I thought he was talking about the police sketch, but that didn't make sense. Why would he need the sketch anyway? The police sketch was already out on the wires when . . .

Unless it was to protect someone?

That didn't make sense either. No one had known about it. It had been in the hands of the CIA since the day I drew it—

The blood does drain out of your face when you receive a severe shock. Someone besides me had seen the sketch.

Willis.

He'd wanted the sketch. Asked for it repeatedly.

He called the round headed man Bobby that night.

Good cop. Bad cop.

He and Dillon had been seriously miscast in their roles.

I reached for the telephone by my bed, but the door opened.

"Hello, Miss Stanley," Detective Willis said from the doorway. He walked in like he had a perfect right, letting the door swing shut behind him. He saw the sketch book in my hand and stopped. His eyes narrowed dangerously.

"So it didn't get blown up in your car. Pity." He came to me, snagged my chin and lifted it. His examination was cold and clinical. "You've put it together, I see."

"The round-headed man said something to me about it at

the convention center." My voice sounded distant, but calm. My brain knew that Willis must have planted the bomb and shot up my pillows, but it hadn't yet made that final link with the place where panic lived.

"Yeah, he told me about that." The smile Willis produced was friendly, regretful, if I didn't look at his dead, cold eyes. "Too bad I have to kill you. I like you. You've got a lot of spunk."

He said it matter-of-factly, not at all like someone delivering a death sentence.

"You'll have to get dressed. You do what I say, don't give me trouble, I'll make it easy for you."

What a prince. What an optimist. I glared at him. "I won't dress in front of you."

He rolled his eyes, checked the bathroom, then gestured for me to go inside. "Hurry up."

Sure. I was gonna hurry to my own death. I got a grip on the back of my hospital gown and slid out of bed. The bathroom door was one direction, the door to my guard the other.

Willis noted my look, shook his head. "He's taking a break."

There was little satisfaction in being right and Kel being wrong about my safety. If Willis got his way, I'd never get the chance to tell him, "I told you so." I couldn't let myself think about all the other things I wouldn't be doing if Willis succeeded, not if I wanted to have a chance to stop him.

There was no lock on the door, so I dressed quickly, then did a quick search of the far too sterile bathroom. All I turned up was a bar of soap, a bottle of Phisohex and a toothbrush.

Great, I could disinfect him to death. I used the soap to write "Help" and "Willis" on the mirror, then shoved the Phisohex in my pocket. I knew from personal experience it could cause pain.

Willis beat on the door. "What's taking you so long?"

I opened the door. "I'm a little nervous about dying, okay?"

"Like I said, you got spunk." He grabbed my arm and shoved me towards the door. "Just don't get carried away with it."

I didn't look back. I'd given it my best shot. Now I had to concentrate on warding off Willis' best shot until the cavalry came. I just hoped the pissed off cavalry didn't think I'd run off with Jerome again. Hard not to think about the story of the boy who cried wolf one too many times.

In the movies, potential victims try to get their killers to talk. It was practically obligatory. The killers seem to like this, so when he pushed me into the parking garage elevator and let me go, I decided to try it.

I rubbed my arm where he'd gripped it and said accusingly, "You're supposed to be a good guy."

He shrugged. "I happen to think I still am, in my way."

"Your way? By selling guns to terrorists? By killing boys, math teachers, and innocent authors for filthy gain?" I didn't mention his murder of the round-headed man. It weakened my case.

"This isn't about money." His response was quick and defensive. Had I found a weak spot?

"Oh? You're killing out of the goodness of your heart? Or, let me guess. You have a great cause?"

He looked annoyed. "It's too bad I missed you Saturday. You got a smart mouth."

"So, what am I dying for?"

"You wouldn't understand anymore than the Carter broad did." He frowned. "Damn Bobby to hell for overreacting."

"I suppose he killed Paul Mitchell because he noticed armament was missing?"

He looked at me. I didn't like the look and had to swallow a great wad of fear.

"You've found out quite a bit for a 'harmless' author."

"Maybe not so harmless as you think. I found the papers Mrs. Carter took, they were in a typewriter. The CIA has them now. They know about the embassies. So it's all been for nothing." I watched him carefully as I hauled out the tried and true bluff.

"Clever old broad. We wondered . . ."

"We?"

He smiled slowly. "Why, me and Bobby, of course."

"You're going to die. Just like he did. They know everything. Kel told me—"

"Your spook doesn't know shit. He could walk up and lean on it and he still wouldn't know shit. I didn't start this, you know. They did." His face darkened, his eyes taking on a weird glow that sent a series of tremors down my spine. "With their power brokering. If they'd listened. But they never do, not unless you got the money. After Tuesday . . ."

He stopped, as if afraid he'd say too much.

"Listen to what?"

"Why," he smiled, suddenly, "the second shot to be heard around the world."

I frowned. I knew about the first shot. I was a teacher, but what could a revolutionary war shot have to do with now? Was that it? Was he talking revolution? Now? When we were in the midst of a war?

The elevator doors slid open, spewing us into the shadowy, empty depths of the parking garage. A chill that had nothing to do with the outside cold, numbed my body and my brain as he hauled me across the concrete towards a silver Datsun.

So he was responsible for that, too. The bastard.

He shoved me into the space between the cars and pulled a pair of handcuffs out of his pocket.

"Gimme your hands."

If I let him handcuff me, the pathetically little chance I had of escaping dwindled into that negative, new math range. I hated new math. Hate put an extra spin on the old brain, the little ball landing in the Phisohex slot.

"What are you going to do?" I half turned away from him and slipped the bottle out of my pocket, my thumb working at the stiff top.

"I don't want any trouble from you. Think I can't see the wheels turning? Now put 'em out."

I let my shoulders droop in defeat. Stepped towards him, lifting my hands, palms down so that he wouldn't notice the bottle. When his gaze dropped to my wrists, I turned the bottle and squeezed—just as cold steel snapped into place around my wrists.

My cry of dismay got lost in his roar of pain. He clawed at his eyes with his free hand. I used his distraction to apply my knee where it would hurt and jumped back as he doubled over with another howl.

For an instant I saw his inflamed eyes, bulging from Phisohex and rage.

I turned tail and ran like a rabbit. Unfortunately I was a handcuffed rabbit, so my gait lacked effective forward motion, being hampered with the side to side swing of my elbows.

The elevator sign glowed like an ugly beacon through the gloom. The light showed it still on our floor.

I tried to pick up my pace. Instead I went side ways and bounced off a parked car. A bullet thudded into the car next to me. I screamed and skittered the other way. Ahead of me, the elevator light went dark.

"No!!!" Oblivious to my plight, it started to descend. My only option was to follow. I leapt over the cement barrier of the down ramp. Behind me bullets ricocheted off metal and concrete. With all the grace of a disadvantaged kangaroo, I galloped down the ramp and made a turn toward the elevator.

Only this level didn't have an elevator.

Above me I heard shambling footsteps and steady cursing. Despite this rare opportunity to enlarge my off-color vocabulary, I continued my ineffective scamper for the next down ramp.

The pounding of my footsteps and heart drowned out his pursuit. I couldn't look back without loosing my balance. All I could do was run and hope.

Several lifetimes later, I reached the next ramp. I went over the low curb and almost came a header on a patch of oil. I kept my balance, but never quite got back control. Several hops and a Beemer put me back on target for the elevator.

The indicator showed it on the first floor—no, it was climbing.

The bastard had taken time to push the button.

I galloped forward.

One. Two. Three . . .

I was almost there—it swept past my floor bare seconds before my fingers found the button and pushed. It went up one level and stopped. After a short silence, I heard Willis' footsteps start toward me.

I pushed the button again. It didn't move.

Could he have blocked it somehow?

I sagged against the wall, my chest heaving its need for more air. I was on the fourth level. There was no way I could run the lengths of four levels to the ground. I had to get back up to the elevator. Or hide until the cavalry came.

If the cavalry came.

A garage didn't offer a whole lot in the way of cover, but if I could convince him I was still headed down, maybe I could work my way back up to the stalled elevator.

I took a deep breath, pushed away from the elevator, and began jogging towards the other ramp, deliberately emphasizing my steps with teeth jarring thumps. It hurt like hell, but I heard his footsteps speed up. When I figured he was making too much noise to hear me, I dodged behind an ancient van with "Wild Thing" inscribed on the side.

It seemed like a good omen.

Sooner than I'd expected, Willis thudded past, his livid face contorted with rage. If he caught me now, he wouldn't make it easy for me. I waited until he was out of sight, then did a crab walk around the front of the van.

Below me, Willis stopped running. I froze. If he'd already realized I wasn't going down, I was toast. Even now he could be silently returning the way he'd come. I had to do something.

I hardly had time to form the prayer in my head when the answer came in a resurrected memory of an action adventure movie from my past. The bulging pectoral hero had clung to the underside of a truck. I didn't have the pecs, but I didn't have to cling to it while the van was moving either. With my hands thoroughly cuffed, it wasn't easy getting under the van and not make noise, but I had good incentive to try. Once there, I focused so much on figuring out how to hook my joined arms around machinery, that at first I didn't realize what I was seeing.

A spare key holder.

If it had a key in it—it did.

Yes, thank you God. Driving out surrounded by lots of metal was much better than cowering in grease while waiting for a cavalry that might not come.

I had the key in the lock when I heard Willis heading back my way. The door squeaked when I opened it, sending my heart and Willis' footsteps racing. I scrambled into the driver's seat, pulled the door closed and locked it. I managed to get the key in the ignition and cranked it. The engine hesitated, then turned over with a satisfying roar. With a painful pretzel of my arms, I got it in reverse.

Willis' face topped the cement curb. It was a fearsome sight. The eyes were red and swollen, the whites bulging out of puffy flesh crisscrossed by angry red scratches dripping blood.

For a terrifying moment we stared across the concrete yards that divided us. He raised his gun. I stamped on the gas. The van shot back. A bullet starred the window of the car next to me. I cranked frantically. A bullet hit the side of the van. Another glanced off the windshield. I hit the brake. The van's tires shrieked a protest, then we slammed into the car parked behind. An alarm went off.

I turned the wheel to straighten the tires. Willis ran into my path and pointed his gun at me.

I closed my eyes and hit the gas. The van leapt forward. Shots. Bullets thudded into metal. Another volley. The van veered right, wresting control from my shackled hands.

A yell. A thump. A lurch. A skid sideways into another car. My head hit the steering wheel. Lights out.

Chapter Twenty-two

Returning light brought pain. Instead of a soft pillow, hard plastic un-gently cradled my head. On the bright side, gentle fingers touched arms, my legs. Who?

Memory wasn't gentle. It slammed into my brain.

Willis. Gun. Death.

I started to struggle. "I have Phisohex!"

"Is that what you did to the poor guy?" The voice sounded like Kel's.

"I told you I wasn't safe in the hospital," I muttered. Death could have me now that I knew he'd live the rest of his life tortured by guilt.

I sagged back and waited. No light beckoned me into the next world, so I opened my eyes. It hurt. I didn't want to do that again, so I left them open and tried out my arms and legs. I didn't think I could be more uncomfortable.

I was wrong.

"You shouldn't move," Kel began.

"No kidding." I tried them again, but slower. They still hurt, but bones didn't grind together. "Can you help me out of here?"

"You should wait for the EMT," Kel said, but he took my cuffed hands and helped me scramble clear of "Wild Thing." Kel looked at the cuffs, gave a low voiced order to a man standing by him, then said. "That explains your driving, but not why you tried to run over Willis."

I gave him a haughty look. "He was going to kill me."

The man dug through the prone Willis, then tossed Kel some keys. Kel started to fit them in the lock, then stopped.

"I think I'll apologize before I unlock you. Phisohex doesn't agree with me either."

I don't know how he did it. Every bone and muscle in my body hurt, including my heart, but my lips still gave this little twitch, like they wanted to smile. The sharp-eyed spy saw this sign of weakness and compounded his crimes with an illegal use of his unregistered smile.

Cheeky.

He undid one side, then the other, his face turning grim when he saw their rubbed raw state. "You know, I've lost ten years off my life for every day I've known you."

"And someone has tried to kill me every one of those days," I said it lightly, with only a little wobble in my voice. "Maybe someone is trying to tell us something."

He was standing close enough to singe, but my flesh didn't seem to care. Every cell strained toward him. It took what was left of my willpower not to let the cells have their wicked way.

"That we're," he didn't touch me, he didn't need to, "good together?"

"I'm sure that must be it." I felt my mouth stretch in a stupidly happy grin. I was insane. I liked it.

I liked basking in the glow of being lusted after by a guy I actually wanted to lust after me. It was like I'd finally figured it out. I'd finally found the right intersection of male wanting and female need. So much of my life had been missed cues and screwed up timing, surely I deserved to bask a little?

Right then, I could have kissed Mrs. MacPhearson for getting the flu. Course, I'd rather have kissed Kel—if all the extraneous cops would just go away.

They didn't. Instead, more came. Some firemen. Another EMT gave me a once-over. I ignored him and looked at Kel with a goofy expression on my face while he tried to act official and ask me some questions. I told him everything I remembered about my abduction and what Willis had said. He looked thoughtful, but didn't say if any of it meant anything. I didn't care if it meant anything. I was so tired I was seeing triple. My body had had enough.

"I want to go home."

He promised to see what he could do, which turned out to be enough. The hospital couldn't make a case for keeping me since I hadn't prospered in their care. The double dose of SWAT team was ruining their healer image, so, after giving me instructions that I didn't listen to, and making me sign a thousand forms, I was released into the custody of my mother and the CIA—in the form of Kel's suits. Kel had a Tuesday deadline for the disaster and had to go.

I spent what was left of my day quietly, watched a bit of the war and worked on my next roach book. Marion wouldn't consider near extinction a reasonable excuse for missing a deadline. As it got towards evening, I shoved a music tape in my player. As Mama Cass began to wail about friends and lovers and was pondering what might be in my refrigerator for eating, I heard a knock at my door.

Most of my guests enter through the main house, so I wasn't too surprised, when I'd grabbed Addison's collar and opened the door, to catch Kel with his government issue lock pick in one hand and holding some bags that smelled Chinese with the other.

It is said one should beware of Greeks bearing gifts and men with etchings, but my mother never told me how to deal with a spy in tight-fitting jeans bearing Chinese food.

So I let him in.

★★★★★

"Eclair?" I held out the nearly thawed treat. I always keep some in my freezer to satisfy sudden cravings. Too bad I couldn't keep Kel there, too. He was rousing all sorts of cravings that needed satisfaction. He accepted the treat, but didn't appear to notice the lust that went with it, as he leaned back in his seat for a bite.

"Aren't you going to have one?" he asked.

"I've been eating my dessert first lately, in case I don't live through dinner," I said. I slid off my stool and started cleaning up, shoving cartons and sacks into the garbage or refrigerator, depending on their state of emptiness. As I worked, I subjected Kel to a discreet study from under my lashes.

If I were a romance heroine with a carefully constructed plot to aid me, this would be sack time. My conservative, Baptist self approached this idea cautiously. This was real life. My life. It was one thing to imagine love scenes between imaginary people. Quite another to become intimate with someone I knew—yet didn't know at all.

Kel got up to help, further disturbing my insides. It unsettled me to stand shoulder to shoulder and wash dishes with him. I kept noticing little things, like the soap bubbles popping on the wet skin of his arm. The way he smelled, a mix of musk, Chinese and chocolate. The shadow of a beard giving texture to smooth jaw line. How comfortable I felt with him even as every inch of my skin tingled with wanting.

I'd seen men roll up their sleeves and wash dishes once or twice in my lifetime. Just this week I'd seen Mike in a robe and had three young bucks in tight jeans lusting after me, none of which affected me like watching Kel in my kitchen, washing my dishes, with no-name soap bubbles on his wet arms.

When he finally dried the last bubble, an activity that shouldn't have made his muscles flex so enticingly, he didn't roll his sleeves back down. Instead, he dropped on my couch and looped his arms behind his head, an action that stretched his shirt disturbingly across his chest. It was a good chest, even with the bandage ruining the smooth line of his muscles. I should know. I'd put it under the microscope of my fingertips.

"What a day," he muttered, rubbing the back of his neck.

"Yeah."

Trying for the same relaxed air, I sank into a chair opposite him, and without thinking, swept a pile of magazines off the coffee table with my foot so I could stretch my legs out. I saw him looking at me with amusement but was too tired to do anything but grin.

He half lifted a foot. "Mind if I join you?"

"Be my guest."

I thought it would be easier, more relaxed across from him, but with his legs stretched out close to mine, his eyes studying me intently, his body "at ease" but still emanating coiled strength, my tension increased instead of decreased.

"So," I nervously cleared my throat, "how's everything going? Have you figured out what's going to happen on Tuesday?"

He rubbed his hair and grimaced. "The shell game. No, not yet. Though I think I'm getting close."

"You still think that someone is to distract you from the real issue?"

"More than ever, after what Willis said. Whoever is behind the con is pretty certain he can keep our focus misdirected until it's too late to do anything about it."

"So the embassies may be part of that misdirection? He didn't seem worried that you'd found that out."

"It could be the embassies themselves, or it could be the method. If they had what they considered a fool proof method of delivery, it could make Willis feel confident. If we could get him to talk—" Kel shrugged.

"He was careful not to tell me too much either, which I thought showed a real lack of trust on his part. Obviously he doesn't watch enough TV. Or watches too much." I was still trying to decide which, when I realized that Kel was looking at me like someone with bad news to deliver.

"Bel?" There was a curious note, too. "I've been looking into Kenyon Business Machines. It was the last place Mrs. Carter went the night she died. To an executive board meeting for her PAC. She had to have stashed the papers in the typewriter that night."

My heart did a funny lurch. If she hid the papers there, was it because she felt threatened there?

I pulled my legs off the table and leaned forward. "You think the Kenyons are involved?"

He shrugged. "I wish I knew. All the clues lead back to the PAC. Elspeth Carter goes to a PAC meeting. She dies, presumably because she found the papers then and hid them. Paul Mitchell dies by the same gun. He's the supply officer for a supply depot missing some important armament. Howard kills him and is killed. Then we find evidence linking him to a terrorist group. Obvious conclusion, terrorists are planning a raid on the embassies highlighted in the papers. Right?"

"Right."

"Except Willis isn't worried that we know this. So I dig a little deeper and I find out that Mitchell was also a member of PT-PAC."

I nodded, remembering my conversation with the lady at the booth. "Don't tell me the round-headed man was a member, too?"

Kel shook his head. "Not a member. But a contributor. A substantial contributor. As was Willis."

"How substantial are we talking about?"

"Hundreds of thousands of dollars."

"How did they pay that kind of money to the PAC? And why would they—if they had that kind of money?"

"Yeah, I'd like the answers to those questions, too. They sure as hell weren't interested in education reform." He looked at me soberly. "Three years ago PT-PAC was about to disband because of a lack of funds. Flynn Kenyon came on board and suddenly they're raking in the cash. But they still don't have any clout. You ever hear of a PAC with money but no politicians?"

"No, but—"

"What?"

"Flynn Kenyon as bad guy? There's no way on this earth—"

"Aren't you forgetting something?"

"What?"

"Where Elspeth Carter hid those papers? She felt threatened at Kenyon's. She hid them there. Now I checked the attendance for that meeting. Neither Willis nor Howard was there. Flynn Kenyon was."

I stared at him. "He's a grandfather."

Kel pulled his long legs clear of the table and sat forward, his elbows propped on his knees, his eyes worried for me. "I'm sorry this is hitting close to home for you."

"It's not just that. Why would a guy who's worried about education blow up embassies?"

He rubbed his face. "I don't know." His eyes looked tired, his face drawn and stroked with gray.

"Now if it was the capital . . ." I said, lightly, hoping to distract him. It couldn't be easy knowing lives were resting on his ability to see which shell was hiding which pea.

"The capital? Why?" he asked, absently.

"What, doesn't the CIA know PT-PAC's current reform effort?" I shook my head in mock reproof. "You obviously don't know the right people to talk to."

"What are you talking about?"

"They've jumped on the term limitation bandwagon. I signed the petition myself at the convention on Friday."

Kel grinned, his whole face lightening. "I guess the Democrats would consider that a form of terrorism, but—" He stopped abruptly, an arrested expression on his face.

"I was joking," I protested, uneasily. He ignored me.

"If I could only see how? That's got to be the key." He stared into the distance for a moment. "Term limitation. What an intriguing concept," he murmured. "There are a lot of ways to limit terms, but the quickest way is—"

"You're not seriously considering . . . no way."

"It's my job to consider possibilities."

"But, I mean, everyone wants to get rid of Congress, but, they're like zits. They only go away if they want to. It's democracy not working. Nobody plots to blow them up."

"Tuesday night is the State of the Union address. They'll all be together in one place at one time."

"But surely people have thought of that? Taken a few precautions? A few Patriot missiles lying around?"

"What if there's something we haven't thought of? Willis was pretty confident."

I felt this tiny bell go off in my head, the one that warns me I'm forgetting something. Unfortunately, all it does is warn me. It doesn't tell me what I'm forgetting.

"I shouldn't have worried you with this." Kel, looking regretful, stood up. "But I needed to pick your brain. You're the one whose been hanging out with the bad boys."

I smiled. Etta Place I was not. "You leaving?"

"I've got to follow up the leads you gave me."

"You're going after the Kenyons, aren't you?" I asked, more to hold him here, than to know. I wanted time to look my fill at the spy who was leaving me.

"Just going to sniff around a bit. Don't want to spook them." Maybe he saw the regret and longing in my eyes because he sighed. He cupped my face with his hands. "I have to go, Bel."

"I know. You have to save Congress . . . I suppose you do have to save them? I mean, they didn't vote for your raise."

It was a feeble joke, but I needed to lighten an atmosphere that was starting to simmer. I swallowed, then licked my lips. He followed the movement intently, a fire starting in his eyes. I don't know who moved first. All that mattered was my mouth and his were together at last. The coffee table kept our bodies apart, but not our passion.

He was chocolate and cream. He was everything nice. Not a hint of puppy dog tails or snails . . .

He tried to step over the coffee table, slipped on the magazines I'd dumped off and tumbled us both onto the sofa, then we slid to the floor. Space was tight, which suited me. We had to stay together to fit. It was hard on elbows as our hands explored each other, but what are elbows in the face of passion?

It was easier for him to breach my robe's boundaries, but I was on the bottom and had more elbow room, so we got to flesh at almost the same time. I wanted to sink into this vortex of passion, but there was something poking into my back.

"Could we . . . there's something in my back," I muttered into his ear. "No. Don't stop . . . just—"

He rolled sideways and the coffee table shrieked across the floor, sending a small shower of papers down on us. But the pain in my back was gone, leaving only the ache for him.

"How's that?"

I rolled on top and gazed down into dimple and blue eyes.

"Perfect. It's perfect."

I bent my head, wanting only to feel his mouth on mine again, but the mood was already dying.

"What's that?" he said, softly, his hands on my body stilling their heady explorations.

"Isabel?" It was my mother and she sounded close, like right outside the door. I heard her fumble with the knob and looked in panic at Kel. There was a flurry of bodies. I still don't know how I made it to my feet before my mother rounded the corner. I finished knotting my robe, while assuming what I hoped was a calm expression.

"Mother." I stole a peek. Kel was on the floor, tucking in his shirt.

"I thought you'd be in bed by now?"

"No." Darn it.

She frowned. "You're awfully flushed. Do you have a fever?"

"No." There was a stealthy slide as Kel worked his way past me. I turned and headed for my bedroom. My mother turned too, giving Kel the diversion he needed.

"Where are you going?"

I felt the brush of cool air across my feet as the door opened and closed, but it didn't cool anything higher. "I'm going to take a cold shower."

"Have you lost your mind?"

"I haven't lost anything tonight, mother. In the morning I'll let you know if that's good or bad. Right now I'm not sure."

Chapter Twenty-three

Despite the metallic gray of the winter sky and the dead grass underfoot, the park looked festive and patriotic when I arrived for my rehearsal with the guys who loved me. Bleachers and a bandstand had been erected near the cement square that now contained the "pig" shrouded in white for it's moment of glory this evening.

Nearby, trees fluttered with hundreds of yellow and white ribbons and men labored to string red, white, and blue steamers on everything that wasn't moving. They were even erecting a flagpole. Obviously a serious patriotic frenzy was in the making.

The guys, now attired in Desert Storm gear and accompanying military swagger, were glad to see me, despite their recent frisking. Or maybe because of it.

As we tweaked and twisted our equipment into emitting weird wailing sounds that eventually steadied into something vaguely musical, I pondered the problem of my young admirers. Though some may dispute it, I am convinced I got a desperately needed bolt of inspiration.

I needed to kiss them.

It was the quickest way to remove their Cosmo-induced curiosity about love with an older woman. And it would help clarify things for me. I hadn't gotten my kiss from Mike because he'd fallen for Rosemary. If they tasted as good as Kel, then I'd know my hormones were having their last hurrah before the onset of menopause and I wasn't falling in love with the spy who kept revving my engine, then leaving me.

I had to wait until after the rehearsal to put thought into action. We did our run through, then learned other details about the ensuing patriotic frenzy, like the fact that there were three parks, three rallies, and three pigs to receive dedicating, but we were the only ones who got to have Lee Greenwood.

The other rallies would have to watch him on a big screen by satellite. We were also the only ones to get CNN.

Rehearsal completed, I turned my attention back to the problem of how to lure three young men into kissing me. Inspiration struck again. Obviously God wanted me to kiss these boys. All I had to do was sing the "Little Mermaid" song about "kissing the girl" before we closed up shop. And if that didn't work? Well, if they could read Cosmopolitan to develop sensitivity, and then not develop any, then I didn't want to kiss them.

Like the Sirens of myth, I started slow and let it build, luring them with words and song. Fortunately, they appeared to have acquired the needed sensitivity. Drum and Tommy did fast, good work, their technique suited to their individual personalities. Unfortunately, my knees stayed steady as a rock, but I did learn a thing or two for my book.

Jerome made me work for it. Of course, there was a marriage proposal still on the table between us. I smoothed the desert tan tee shirt wrinkling slightly across one broad shoulder and gave him what I hoped was an inviting look from under my lashes.

"What's the kiss supposed to prove?" he asked, his voice going husky, but still laden with amusement.

No wonder I liked the boy.

"Well, I figured if we . . . kissed and then we, well, felt like singing or something, then I . . . we'd know."

"Singing? Like a love song?"

"I'm not looking for a dance number here."

"You've been watching too many musicals. Any particular song you got in mind?" Amusement came out into the open in his eyes.

I started to smile, too. "I was thinking of something smoky and edged with jazz, but since you're a white boy, I won't hold it against you if you can't."

He laughed. "You're something else, Stanley."

He looked at for me for a moment, then stepped up to the mound, so to speak. His lips settled over mine, pleasant, nice tasting, sweeping away the present, and Kel from my thoughts, carrying me back in time. I was sixteen again and getting my first kiss. The kind of kiss I'd been hoping for from Freddie Frinker and hadn't gotten. I even got a little wobble in my knees. But it didn't knock them out from under me the way Kel's kisses did. And there was no music.

"Sweet Sixteen" didn't count.

"What now?" Jerome asked, still looking amused and ever so slightly regretful. I guess he could read the writing on my lips as well as the next guy.

"I think we stay friends. It's the way they do it in all the best musicals," I said, with a few regrets of my own.

It was a relief, though, so we kissed on it again, only friendly this time, though Jerome tried to take advantage by stretching it out a bit. I let him because of Freddie and the spit rainbow, then watched him swagger away, wondering if I should have tried a little harder to get that song going in my heart—

"Are you finished?"

I really did need to stop meeting Kel like this.

He was several feet away and glaring, but my stupid knees

still went soft, just from remembering what it was like to kiss him. There was obviously more going on than hormonal hurrahs, but I wasn't ready to admit what that might be. There was too much risk, too much possible pain following that path to its natural and logical conclusion.

The sun glanced off the burnished brown of his hair, the highlights winking as the wind ruffled the surface. His skin glowed from the fresh air and he had on this truly great coat.

He slipped sunglasses over the glare and walked, no stalked, over to me.

I crossed my arms, determined not to feel guilty for conducting what was essentially scientific research. On his behalf. "What do you want now?"

"I want you to look at something."

Etchings?

"The computer sheets you found."

Oh, well. Baptist girls weren't supposed to look at etchings anyway. "Why?"

"There's some handwriting on one of them that I want you to see if you recognize. Do you mind?"

"No, I don't mind."

Despite my agreement, he didn't move. I shoved my hands, cold now that I was no longer kissing boys, into my coat pockets.

Kel looked around. "So, what's going on here?"

"Going on?" I slid on my dark glasses, why should all the advantage be his?

"Yeah. All this stuff. The ribbons, bandstand—"

"It's a rally in support of the troops. And they're dedicating a pig."

Kel's brows arched above the top of his glasses, telling me he was startled. "Pig?"

I pointed at the howitzer. "Pig. It has this military

sounding name, but Flynn just calls it the pig."

"Flynn? Flynn Kenyon?" Kel asked, sharply. "He's involved in this rally of yours?"

"Actually I'm involved in this rally of his, in a very minor way." I stared at him. He looked tense. "What?"

"Nothing." He nodded towards his car, parked at the edge of the grass. "Let's go. I have the papers in my car."

He took my arm for the walk to his car, but I noticed that several times he looked back at the pig. At the car, he opened the door.

"Get in."

"Are we leaving?"

"I thought we could look at the papers over lunch. I still owe you one. And you did say you were through kissing every guy that happens to walk by."

"I didn't kiss every guy that walked by. Just three of them." I crossed my arms, feeling kind of Schwarztcoff-ish in my Desert Storm gear. "What about my dog?"

"Your dog?" He looked at Addison, frolicking with some children. "Can't he stay and play? He won't fit in my car."

"We've established your car is small, haven't we?"

He started beating a tattoo with his fingers on the top of the small car. "And your dog is big as a horse. But I think Dobbs and Henderson can take him home." He signaled to my watch-suits.

"I suppose so, just warn them to keep him away from your car until we leave."

Kel got kind of immobile. "Why?"

He laid a protective hand on his car.

"He likes to bite off the mirrors."

"He—why?"

"I think he's patriotic and believes people should buy American."

Kel pulled rank on the suits. We left without Addison and with his side mirrors intact, though it was a near thing. We sped rapidly away from the park, traveling in silence for several blocks before Kel took up the attack again.

"So, did you give Jerome his answer?" He sounded a little too noncommittal.

"Yes."

"Before or after the long kiss."

I smiled. "It wasn't that long—the light is green now—isn't it kind of hard on your transmission to grind the gears like that?"

He accelerated rapidly, deliberately abusing his transmission again. "Every time I turn around you're getting cozy with those boys."

"Not every time. It was a practice."

"Is that what you call it? Sounded more like soliciting to me." I liked the aggrieved edge to his voice. If I had to be baffled, then he should be aggrieved. "It's dangerous to encourage them like that. Young men's hormones, well, they can get out of hand."

"Really?" He ground his teeth, so I added soothingly, "Actually I was trying to discourage them."

"I don't think it worked."

"They were just high on the idea of liking me. I removed the mystery—"

"Mystery?"

"Yeah. I think they thought it would be, like amazing to kiss me or something. I disabused them of the idea and now we're all just good friends again."

"They didn't think kissing you was amazing?" He pulled through the light and stopped in front of the same Mexican restaurant where we'd been shot at before.

"No." I turned to look at him, found myself nose to nose

with him. He removed his glasses, then mine and snared me in the glow of his hot, blue gaze.

"I find that hard to believe." His voice husky, he leaned close, his hand sliding over mine nestled in my lap and lifted it to his mouth.

All I could do was stare, the breath stealing from my lungs in a gentle whoosh as his mouth slid across the back of my hand.

"Oh." It was not brilliant, but it was all I could manage. I started to lean towards him, surrender in my heart. Apparently he didn't want it. He turned and slid out of the car. I watched him walk around to open my door, pique replacing passion.

Again he had failed to take advantage of a lady in the front seat of his car? The man wasn't doing his part to improve the CIA's bad image.

I managed to drown my pique in the excellent lunch. Feeling mellow and much more forgiving, I leaned forward, pushing aside my water glass, my hand idly playing with the petals of the flower that drooped in the center of the table as we chatted about everything but what brought us together.

Kel leaned forward, linking his hand with mine, both our elbows on the table, we stared at each other across the minimal space, like arm wrestlers waiting the starting gun—

The thought must have formed in both our minds at the same time. Instantly we were straining, turning our table into a mini-battle field of the sexes. Of course I lost. I hadn't been rigorously trained by the government. But sometimes losing can be winning. With my arm down on the table, our faces ended up just millimeters apart.

He shortened the distance. I let him, fluttering my lashes down on my cheeks in what I hoped were alluring half-moons. But instead of kissing me he jumped to his feet like he'd heard a gunshot.

"Mother!" His hand went to his tie.

For one awful moment, I thought it was my mother. Then it hit me. I jerked back from my draped position on the table and knocked over my water glass.

"What are you doing here?" He tugged his tie again. I didn't blame him. His mother was flawlessly turned out.

I saw her attention turn toward me and braced for it, but her eyes were as clever as Kel's at disguising what she was thinking.

"You played at Ellie's funeral," she said, her voice as coolly elegant as her dark suit. She looked like the perfect political wife, but probably wasn't with a name like Kapone. I braced for a more polite form of my mother's dismay, but she startled me by adding, "It was lovely. You've been to New Orleans?"

"I taught school there for several years," I admitted.

Mrs. Kapone slanted a look at her son that was both charming and mischievous. He blushed. A real, honest-to-goodness blush.

"Kel had the most darling crush on Ellie . . . Elspeth Carter when he was ten," she confided. "That's how we met. She invited me in to discuss a poem—"

"Mother!" Kel protested.

I found myself exchanging an amusing, faintly superior female look with Kel's mother. I will confess I didn't just enjoy it, I reveled in it.

She left us to finish our business, with an admonition to Kel to come home for Sunday dinner this weekend. He kissed her cheek, murmured something soothing, but noncommittal, then escorted her to a seat with her friends.

When he'd rejoined me, he managed to avoid making eye

contact by pulling the computer sheet from his inside jacket pocket. Instead of serious spy, he looked sort of boyish. I knew how he felt. When your mother was watching, it just didn't matter how old you were. All that mattered was how old you felt.

I was thinking how endearing he was until a movement gave me a glimpse of the gun nestled inside his jacket. It was a timely reminder of who and what he was.

This wasn't just the man I'd most like to kiss. This wasn't just a man with a truly classy mother who could be as embarrassing as my mother. This was a CIA agent. A man who carried a gun and who used it in the service of his country. I'd seen him shoot it. He'd probably killed with it.

A girl who got mixed up with him was likely to find herself featured on a made-for-television movie of the week. I should look at the stupid computer sheets and then hie me back to my roach as quickly as I possibly could. I was out of my league.

In pursuit of this goal, I asked, "Kel, you don't still think the Kenyons are mad plotters, do you?"

He paused in the act of unfolding the sheet. "I don't know about the elder Kenyon. I know his son, Dag, is not squeaky clean."

This did not surprise me.

"He was in debt past his eyeballs, until last month. He suddenly paid the worst of his debts off with money from an overseas account. The FBI is still trying to trace where it came from. If we'd got on to him sooner—" He shrugged.

"The bum. He cries poverty to Rosemary all the time." Though he had offered a cash payment for the Mercedes, I remembered, and smiled. "Kel! He was at the convention, when the round-headed man came after me! It was him. The lousy, bast—ahem."

"I did wonder how Howard found out you were there. Couldn't find the link between him and Willis for that one." He leaned towards me. "The pieces are starting to fit together, particularly . . ."

He stopped, then held up the sheet. "Remember I told you these were schematics for embassies?"

I nodded.

"Well, they're more than that. They're printouts from a pretty sophisticated computer modeling program."

"Really? To do what?"

"To analyze the structure of certain buildings for weaknesses. The military uses something similar to study the impact of missiles and artillery shellings on different types of buildings. The idea being to find the best place to aim your device to bring it all down."

I didn't like what I was hearing. "Are you telling me that someone—" Not someone. Dag "—has been analyzing the Israeli and Egyptian embassies so he can shoot missiles at them?"

"That's what it looks like. If you can identify the handwriting on this sheet, well, I might have enough to pull him in for questioning."

"But this, you're saying this could link him to those terrorists you were talking about? The ones buying the weapons?"

"If what I suspect is true, they haven't just been selling weapons to them. They've been helping the terrorists choose targets and set them up for an attack."

"But that doesn't make any sense. Why would they betray their country . . ." Money. With Dag it was always about money. Except Willis. He said it wasn't the money. "Willis doesn't think he's betraying his country, Kel."

"It's the shell game. What if each component of the plot has their own agenda? And something, perhaps their final objective, has dovetailed together? We've got Kenyon hard up for cash. We got some crooked guardsman with weapons to sell. We've got some people with a political agenda they want to hurry up. And we've got some terrorists who want to cause chaos in this country. I've put together a scenario, where all these elements could work together. If the last piece fits."

He didn't say what that piece was.

"Have you seen Kenyon hanging around the park where your rally is being held?"

I shook my head. "Just Flynn has been around. But I suppose Dag could be at one of the other sites."

"Other sites?"

"Yeah, there's going to be three simultaneous rallies tonight. CNN is going to broadcast from ours when Greenwood does his big number."

"Three rallies? Will there be three guns?"

I nodded. "Does it matter?"

"Three. I didn't think . . ." He stared straight ahead for a long moment, his gears obviously turning, then he spread the sheet out for me to look at. "Here's the notations. Do you recognize the handwriting?"

I reluctantly bent over the sheet. I wasn't eager to finger my nieces and nephew's father conspiring against the government of the United States. But when I saw it, I could feel the blood drain from my face.

"Bel? What's wrong? Isn't it Kenyon's?"

"It's *a* Kenyon. But not Dag's." I looked at Kel in shock. "It's *Muir* Kenyon's handwriting!" Talk about mind boggling.

"Muir? That's the other son. Are you sure? How come you recognize his handwriting?"

I smiled weakly, my gaze sliding away from his. "We sometimes . . . sort of . . . date."

Kel looked resigned. “Of course you do.”

A distraction seemed in order. “I wonder if this is the computer program he’s been trying to show me all week?”

Chapter Twenty-four

Despite my deficiencies as a sleuth, I was bright enough to be worried after my lunch with Kel. I didn't have the resources of the CIA at my disposal or all the clues laid end to end for me to follow. I did know enough to be profoundly uneasy when Kel's suits gave me a ride, through a night already cold and dark, to the park with the pig.

It didn't help my unease that the suits' preppie look had been traded in for ominous form-fitting black jumpsuits, bullet-proof vests and stocking caps. They lacked only the blacking on their faces to be a mini rally invasion force.

In honor of the mood, the radio provided the right background by wailing "Bad Moon Rising."

As we pulled up next to the park, the area marked out for the rally was a brilliant, larger-than-life, splash of light in the otherwise dark park. Spot lights were positioned at the base of the trees festooned with yellow ribbons. The cold breeze sliding through bare branches made the big bows dance and weave like drunken sailors.

My non-suits melted into frenzy's shadow. I wished I could go with them. Since I couldn't, I donned the military sun glasses Flynn insisted we wear with our gear, and quickly found I was glad for them. The contrast of light and dark was as extreme as political ideology and about as painful. Inside the magic circle, the guys moved around the equipment in their desert camouflage, their breath condensing into cloudy puffs around their heads as they exchanged quips.

I stopped at the edge of light overcome by the sensation that something momentous was about to happen. My nerve endings felt charged, my senses super alert as I studied the patriotic scene.

Like ants drawn to the hive, people flowed into the stands from all directions. Some faces I recognized. Reverend Hilliard seated next to Mrs. MacPhearson, pale despite the cold nipping cheeks and nose. Illness had taken the curve out of her robust cheeks, but she clutched a tiny American flag in her fist that she waved periodically.

My family wasn't here. My mother claimed a desire to hear the State of the Union address kept her away. Right. She just didn't want to see me on stage with my boys.

I didn't see Steve, but that didn't mean he wasn't here. He had that strict sense of duty to country that might overcome distaste. No Kenyons in sight either. This was a relief. I didn't know if I was a good enough actress to look them in the eye and pretend I didn't know they were consorting with terrorists and murderers.

I still couldn't get over the idea that poor old Muir was a conspirator, too. I tried to picture him hunched over his computer plotting the trajectory that would take out an embassy, but I couldn't picture him at all. Easier to pull up a picture of the white walls of my hospital room than his face.

I climbed on stage and found that someone had moved my keyboard to the very back of the stage, almost out of sight behind a couple of amplifiers. I thought it was odd, but was actually grateful. This was a bigger crowd than I was used to playing for and I was feeling a bit overwhelmed by everything.

Despite, or maybe because of the cold, the crowd didn't need much of our pre-rally warm-up to reach near frenzy for the arrival of the big-wigs in long, dark limos.

They were exactly on time. It wasn't like bigwigs, but perhaps we were all slaves to CNN and the President's schedule.

I tensed momentarily when Flynn mounted the stand, but he didn't seem to notice me ensconced behind my keyboard at the back of the action and I was able to relax. I studied him, trying to find the evil lurking beneath his saintly exterior. No sign of Dag, which was a huge relief, whether he was a mad plotter or not.

The colors were presented to the sound of a single bugler playing "The Star Spangled Banner." The crisp cold gave each note a clarity that brought tears to my eyes and made the hand over my heart more than a peer pressure induced gesture. In the bold, bright light Old Glory rose on the new flagpole, the breeze whipping it straight. Red, white and blue against the night sky brought a collective sigh from the audience. The music faded into the night and everyone sat down.

It was time for the "hot air." The political speeches passed surprisingly fast, like everyone was set on fast forward. It was odd, but I didn't dwell on it. Lee Greenwood stepped forward and it was time to make some music. In concert with my boys, I keyed the opening notes of "I'm Proud to be an American," the song that had become the rallying cry for the whole war.

Something about the intense cold, brilliant light and heightened emotion brought it all into sharper focus, giving everything a clarity and precision that cut through preoccupation like a Ginzu knife. It was as if my mind had unconsciously been taking notes, and now began sending questions for my conscious mind to ponder.

Questions like, why were the lights angled to cause pain if the audience didn't look directly towards the bandstand?

Why was the memorial pig not in the lime light? All I could see was the very end of its muzzle. The base and rear were completely shrouded in darkness.

The angle of the barrel was odd, too. Shouldn't it be pointing up more, rather than straight down the channel created by the facing bleachers?

Thinking of bleachers, why were they facing each other, instead of the bandstand?

I kept singing and playing on cue, but my mind was a vulture circling the scene before finally settling on Flynn.

He looked relaxed. Too relaxed. He looked at his watch, then at the rear of the pig. So I looked at the rear of the pig. Couldn't see squat with the dark glasses on, but I looked. My hands faltered slightly on the song. No one seemed to notice. Only the words mattered.

I'm proud to be an American.

Flynn was as proud of this country as anyone I knew. It didn't fit for him to throw in with terrorists. Could he be Dag's pawn? That sure fit. Dag was pond scum.

I frowned fixedly into the shadow, hitting about half the keys I was supposed to, and found I could see the dark outline of the pig if I took care not to look into a spotlight. That's when I saw a flicker of movement so slight I wondered if I'd imagined it. Okay, so someone was back there. Made sense. Someone had to unveil the pig.

—going to be something happen today, possibly tonight. It might involve embassies—

—schematics that determined weak spots—

—look right at it and not know what it was—

—second shot heard round the world?

I tensed and just stopped myself from hitting a wrong note. My hands quit moving as my mind sped along the track of clues strewn right and left and added in what Kel had told me, mixed with what I'd learned from war watching.

Artillery was hard to defend against, almost impossible, in

fact, unless you stopped it before launch.

Power brokering.

Shots heard round the world.

I couldn't get that phrase out of my head.

Not while sitting here staring at a pig with a potentially big bang.

If it was pointed in the right direction.

Was it?

I did a mental survey, added in the north and south.

If I was right, the pig was pointed right at the capital building where most of our government was assembling right now.

No. It couldn't be, could it? No one would be insane enough to fire this little piggie from the park.

Not when we were at war.

Surely they weren't that crazy?

I looked at Flynn and caught him looking at his pig. That's when I knew, don't ask me how, that he was that crazy. They were going to fire the pig. If they succeeded, the shot would be heard round the world. No question about it.

As if he heard me thinking, he looked my way and I knew that he knew I knew.

He wasn't just trying to limit the whole of Congress's terms, he'd been part of the attempts on my life.

I arched my brows questioningly, then looked quite deliberately away. There was nothing he could do to me now. Not with the world watching. The real problem was, what could I do about what I knew?

Drum did this riff, startling me out of my thoughts. I hadn't played a note for a whole verse and no one had noticed. Dang Flynn and his plots. I turned to glare at him. Only he wasn't there to glare at. Where did he go?

I looked right.

I looked left.

I should have watched my back.

Someone grabbed my legs and tipped me off the back of the platform. My wounded arm scraped the side and I was out before my head hit the grass.

Millions of kids were having recess inside my head. Jumping. Running. Screaming.

No. That wasn't right. I didn't teach young minds, I twisted them with my roach.

Headache. Not kid-ache. Ouch, arm hurt, too.

I opened my eyes. Dark. Could see grass. Why was grass up my nose. Tried to push it away. Arms weren't working.

Where—oh yeah. Bless the USA. I could hear him singing somewhere off to my right. Couldn't have been out long.

Out? Why was I lying in the grass and not playing?

Various gears in my head turned, inviting more children to rampage through my head, but eventually bringing up a memory of getting grabbed.

Thwacked arm. Bright lights. No light.

Bastards.

I sent the brain kiddies home, but could do nothing about the headache they left. The grass was another story. I went to brush it away and realized I was handcuffed. Again.

It pissed me off. Bad enough getting cuffed by the cops, but when the bad guys did it to me twice, well I'd just had it. At least my hands were cuffed in front. I used my elbows and cautiously lifted my head. The light wasn't good, but I seemed to be lying between the two wheels right under the pig.

I didn't need to know the science of recoil to find this disturbing, not after what I'd observed on the tube.

I inched cautiously sideways, in the direction of the stand and bleachers, but froze when I sensed, rather than saw stealthy movement. Dark, menacing silhouettes against darker shadow moved in and out of my limited view. Once I saw eye whites, more than once the gleam of moonlight off a weapon briefly relieving malevolent silhouettes.

Terrorists.

I was a prisoner of terrorists.

Talk about defying the odds. Did this mean my chances of getting married had just gone up? Or down?

Would I live long enough to find out?

Above the rising crescendo of Greenwood blessing the USA, I heard Flynn's agitated voice.

"You can't do this, Dag!"

"I think you'll find I can." The cool contempt in Dag's voice sent a chill down my prone spine. "What do I care about one tin pot president when there's twenty million dollars on the table?"

"This isn't about money! It was never about the money! You can't kill the president now, while there's a war on!"

"Lighten up, old man. You can bet that whatever Cabinet member stayed home tonight won't mind waking up president of this great land."

It didn't make me happy to have my suspicions confirmed, though it was nice to know I hadn't completely misjudged Flynn. He wasn't a complete villain, just the parent of one. And what was Muir in all this?

As if he'd caught my thought, Flynn asked Dag, "Is your brother in it with you?"

Dag gave a bitter laugh. "Hardly. We both know he wouldn't have stood by and let us kill the delectable Isabel."

Delectable? Perhaps he wasn't a total villain. Maybe ninety-nine percent with just a tiny corner of surprisingly good taste. Or really bad vision. Who can say?

"No," Flynn said, sadly. "And I shouldn't have."

Nice to know who your friends were. Who'd have thought that beneath Muir's dull exterior lurked a knight errant's heart beating just for me?

A pity I was learning too late that appearances are deceiving. Not too late though, I wondered, with a sudden pang. Did they think they had finished me off? No, I answered my own question. You don't cuff dead people. Had I missed the disposition of my person, or was that the topic to come?

"It's too late to turn squeamish now, pater," Dag drawled. "She should have kept her nose out of our business."

"You shouldn't have grabbed her. There was nothing she could have done this late in the game."

"Except point the finger at us," Dag said, turning my way abruptly.

I played possum, though I wanted to lash out when I felt his fingers on my pulse.

"Is she dead?" Flynn asked.

"Not yet."

The chill turned to an ice flow.

"Dag—"

"Don't try to stop me! I owe her for the car and I mean to collect payment in full." I almost cried out when his fingers twisted into my hair. Survival won out over pain, though it wasn't easy. Luckily for me, his interest quickly turned when another figure approached and said something in a low voice.

"Later, my sweet," he said in a low voice, then straightened. "Show time."

"I won't let you do this, Dag." Flynn sounded determined.

"You can't stop me, old man." Dag sounded ruthless. "Cuff him, Hamid."

"I will kill him," a voice I presumed belonged to Hamid

said. I heard Flynn give a muffled groan, but felt no satisfaction. How much worse it must be for him to know his own son had betrayed him.

"No! I want him to see it first. Then you can kill him." Dag moved to the rear of the pig. "Pity Isabel isn't awake to appreciate the irony."

"Irony?" Flynn's voice sounded stifled, filled with pain.

"You don't find it ironic that you'll both die because you tried to save Congress?"

Here I'd thought things were as bad as they could be. He really was worse than a bastard. For once I cursed my Baptist vocabulary that left me without a vile enough epitaph to spit at the scum bag.

"Dag," Flynn's voice sounded strained. "You can still stop this. Fire now, before the President gets there!"

He gave another muffled grunt. I saw a shadowy Hamid raise what looked like an Uzi and bring down on the head of a slumped figure. Dag said nothing.

"Three minutes," another guttural voice intoned.

In my mind I could see the slow sweep of the second hand tracking around the circle of numbers, moving closer, inexorably closer to ground zero. One thousand . . . two thousand . . . I didn't want to count, but I couldn't seem to stop myself.

"Isabel, if you're playing possum down there, you might want to cover your ears. I'm told the blast will be rather loud."

I didn't dignify that with an answer. Against the dark sky and earth, I thought I saw a darker figure rise, move toward us, and then sink into shadow again.

Of course, my suits-out-of-suits were out there somewhere. Kel might be out there, too.

"I know you're awake, Isabel. I can feel you shooting daggers at me," Dag sounded amused. He said something softly, and hands grabbed me, dragged me roughly out from under the pig.

I didn't mind this, because I figured being in the recoil zone of the pig might not be good for my health. I did mind being thrust close to Dag. He patted my cheek. I jerked my head away, though my captor wouldn't let me jerk my body away.

"It won't work. I've watched the war. Artillery isn't that accurate."

Dag's teeth gleamed white in the dark as he smiled. "Then you'll also know the significance of laser guided shells, kissing cousins to the smart bombs they're using. We even have men in position at the targets to guide them in with hand-held targeting lasers. It's quite simple, brilliant, really. Let me give the credit where it's due."

He made a mocking half bow towards Flynn.

I was going to die, probably in a really yucky way, but I still had to say it. "Smart shells to blow up Congress. Isn't that, like, overkill?"

Dag gave a surprised laugh. "Down, but not quite out. I'll have to see what I can do about that when the President's been blown sky high."

"One minute," the time keeper intoned.

Dag turned away from me. All eyes were on the barrel of the pig. In my mind I could see the second hand sweeping toward ground zero. Where was the CIA? Surely they weren't going to choose this moment to screw up?

Behind us Lee Greenwood's voice rose triumphant. Disheartening to know I wasn't missed or needed. Hamid paced towards the pig, his hand reaching eagerly for the mechanism that was to bring the imperialist Americans to their knees—

Suddenly some of the lights shifted blindingly on our little group around the pig. A voice boomed out of the dark,

"Don't anyone move! Do not move—"

I didn't move. The terrorist holding me did. The sound of the shot had barely sounded when he dropped like a rock.

A low swell from the people in the bleachers rose against the finale. The music faltered, the big finish losing it's momentum in the face of this unplanned for federal distraction.

"Lay down your weapons and move away from the howitzer or we will open fire!" The voice was disembodied, metallic, emotionless, but chillingly emphatic. I couldn't tell if it was Kel. It didn't sound like him, but I'd never heard him through a loud speaker.

Hamid moved. Another shot rang out. He slumped into the dark, dead grass. Now there were a few screams from the stands, a sense of stirring, panic waiting to be ignited.

"Anyone who approaches the howitzer will be shot. Lay down your arms and put your hands on top of your heads!"

"It's over." Flynn, slumped against the ground with a bruise swelling on his right temple, looked accusingly at his son. "You screwed up again."

Dag looked like a man who'd just lost twenty million dollars. And been disowned. I had no inclination to feel sorry for him.

The terrorists bent to comply.

At that moment the lights went out.

Not just the rally lights. Everything for several blocks. Houses. Street lights. Utter blackness.

I heard a half scream of fright. A yell of, "Fire!"

Then the acrid smell of smoke.

Panic moved faster than patriotism through the crowd. I heard some shouted pleas for calm, but the sound system had gone down with the lights.

This seemed like a good time for me to become an ex-hostage of terrorists, but before I could make my move, someone grabbed me again. Hope came first. Kel had grabbed me quite a lot this week. Now would be a good time to reprise the grabbing.

Hope got dashed when Dag said in my ear, "You're going to help me get out of here, love. Or die with me."

I didn't like door number one or door number two.

"You're going to kill me anyway," I reminded him. Not because I wanted to, you understand. It was a Ploy. I was stalling.

"There's a lot of ways to die, love."

"So I've been told." I wasn't surprised he was plagiarizing, just that he was doing it with bad dialogue. "Several times just this week."

He gripped my sore arm and jerked. It hurt so bad, I couldn't cry out. I hated the whimper that made it past my lips. Hated him for forcing it out of me.

An official voice gave commands over a bull horn, getting more emphatic, as the crowd became more panicked. In the dark I could hear the sounds of hundreds of feet against the wooden seat of the bleachers, cries for help, and shouts as officials tried to restore calm, the rising swell of a crowd out of control.

Dag used the confusion to drag me towards the bandstand. I didn't resist. Pain was still sending barbed wire tracks back to my brain. And there's something very persuasive about an Uzi in your kidneys.

The cries got louder. There were shots. He pushed me against the bandstand, adding stars to wheel above the barbed wire.

I could feel his cornered-rat panic as he looked for an out using a woman for a shield. The coward.

Then, when I thought things couldn't possibly get any weirder, they did.

Lights came back on. Not normal lights. Strobe lights.

Instead of providing illumination, they added to the confusion, turning the manic multitude—lightly interspersed with terrorists—into a jerky, slow motion frenzy. As a final touch, the fireworks started to go off in bright bursts of patriotic color against the dark, cloudy sky.

No question now whether our rally would make it on CNN tonight. Not even a scud attack would pre-empt this.

"Better late than never," Dag muttered, sounding relieved. "That should cover our retreat. Come on."

He pushed me through the crowd. Ahead of us, Flynn ran into the pack, looking back at the dark figure, with FBI written in light-catching white on his jacket, pursuing him.

He should have been looking forward. Flynn slammed into Mrs. MacPhearson, his body wrapping inexorably around her "S" shaped body. His head got stuck between her massive, pointed breasts. His hands slipped on her polyester coat without finding purchase. They both went down in a tangle of arms and legs and breasts.

Talk about symbolic. The former saint Flynn, sliding around on polyester while Mrs. MacPhearson's dress climbed her hose to expose her cotton knickers for a CNN cameraman.

"Thanks, dad," Dag muttered with a half laugh. Hey, I never said the guy didn't have a sense of humor.

He steered us around his struggling father and shrieking Mrs. M, holding me tight against him as we half-walked, half-trotted towards the street. Jostled by panicked bodies moving weirdly in the midst of strobing lights, inhaling smoke from fireworks and the fire, it all seemed unreal. Like it was a movie and we were just following directions.

"You got a car?"

"I came with the feds." Pissed did a return engagement in

my head. Goons and bad guys had been shooting at me and kidnapping me all week. I was getting tired of it. "Is this a real fire or smoke bomb sleight of hand, Dag?"

"Clever girl. I had a feeling we'd need the time to get away. Only those fools didn't set them off at the right time."

"Maybe you should have synchronized your watches."

Someone bumped into us and Dag's grip tightened. Since I was the one who took the brunt of it on my wounded arm, the ground did a one eighty around me, adding a distinct stagger to my already severely unsteady gait.

"Don't flake out on me now," he said, savagely, giving me another pain spiraling shake.

"Oh, that helped," I muttered as the world did two one-eighties this time. I didn't have to exaggerate the stagger that followed that one, but I did anyway.

I had a Plan. I called it "Pain in the Butt."

I moaned, wobbled, then went limp. It's not as easy as you might think. I mean, all I had was the world's most selfish son of a bitch to catch me.

He did, but only, I suspect, because I was so close I almost took him down with me.

"Damn you! Stand up!"

That did it. I let my knees buckle, let my weight go his way so I could land on him when we went down. Would have worked if someone hadn't broad-sided us from the other direction.

We sprawled untidily in the grass and the Uzi went flying. I was on the bottom. The two on top of me began to grapple and I moved up in the queue to become a kind of victim sandwich, with my head sticking out between two armpits. Someone's belt was digging into my elbow. Someone's elbow was digging into my throat. Both sets of feet were applying bruises to my shins. In one roll I found myself lip to lip with Kel, then another roll put me nose to belly button with Dag.

Not pretty.

After I took a nasty blow to the eye that set off my own private fireworks show, I'd had it with being in the middle.

I applied just enough elbow to a handy solar plexus. When it didn't gasp like Kel, I did it again, only harder. Dag's gasp caused him to retreat enough that I was able to roll over. I hooked my still cuffed hands into the grass and pulled.

It was like being ironed from above and below. Suddenly I was free, breathing, not gasping to get back the air squeezed out of me. The two men rolled close to me, both reaching for the Uzi. I don't know what came over me. I just grabbed it and slammed the butt down on Dag's exposed temple.

No surprise when he immediately went limp.

Kel rolled off him and sat up. Looked at Dag, then at me.

"Nice job," he said. He wiped the blood from the side of his mouth and grinned at me. His face was blacked with whatever it was they used for blacking. Most likely something way more expensive than shoe polish. It was kind of sexy, except I couldn't see his dimple. "You ever considered a career in the CIA? They're looking for a few good women, you know."

"No, I didn't know," I said, sort of bemused as men in black rushed forward, uncuffed me, cuffed Dag instead and hauled him away.

In their wake, more men in black led Flynn, also in cuffs, to a waiting truck. A gap in the crowd revealed Reverend Hilliard, looking somewhat less saintly than before, trying to calm Mrs. MacPhearson.

I felt sorry for him, but not enough to go to a Bible class every Saturday night.

"Can you get up?" Kel asked, recalling my attention. His blue eyes looked even bluer against the black of his skin. I felt like singing hallelujah. Instead, I took the hand he held out, let him pull me up and into his arms.

"We've really got to start meeting like this," I said, while the CNN cameras rolled.

"What the hell were you doing this time?" he asked, stroking the grass from my tangled hair.

"Playing backup for Lee Greenwood?" I answered, brushing the grass from his stocking cap.

He shook his head, grinned, then lifted me off my feet and spun us both in a circle as the fireworks finale lit up in the sky over our heads.

The lady and the spy, together again and on CNN. Surely I could count on them to edit in the fade to the commercial so my mother wouldn't see the clinch?

Then Kel kissed me and I found I didn't care who saw what.

Chapter Twenty-five

The media tried for straight, serious coverage of the pig in Grant Park. There were long shots of the rally with its air of frenzied patriotism, the lights, the shouts, the flags, the people, while blank-faced journalists outlined the events leading up to the mass assassination attempt. It wasn't their fault the copy read like something from National Lampoon.

And when they detailed the Federal agents moving into position barely before the terrorists, their poker-faced delivery only heightened the ludicrousness of the good and the bad lying in the cold practically side by side during the long wait for their differing calls to action.

Lee Greenwood came across well, singing and helping to restore calm in the panic that followed, but the strobe lights, the fireworks, the smoke bombs, and Mrs. MacPhearson's knickers from a variety of camera angles, couldn't play seriously no matter how hard they tried. There was rather a nice shot of me whacking Dag. I cut that one out. And the one of Kel and I kissing.

The confusing plot and counter plot between Dag and Flynn, with its soap opera overtones was, in the end, too complicated for television sound bites. Flynn's evangelical persona, combined with his attempts to "free" the American people from Congressional pork-lock, turned him over night into a folk hero. Instead of ending as near martyrs, Congress ended up with Congressional pie in the face.

A major publisher put up Flynn's bail as an advance against his story and he'd signed the made-for-TV movie rights before the ink could dry on his book contract. Talk show hosts were clamoring for him. Tee shirts, posters, buttons, and bumper stickers with his face popped up everywhere.

There was some criticism, most of it from Congress and directed at the CIA for letting the assassination attempt get so far advanced before stopping it. The rest of the criticism was directed at the CIA for stopping it too soon.

It didn't help that Congress had voted several years earlier to stop funding on an anti-artillery device that would not only have stopped the plot altogether, but saved lives in the Gulf. In the end, no committees were convened to investigate.

Dag and Muir fared less well with the public. Justice had to be served, so justice used them for scapegoats. The role suited them. They looked like criminals, which made it easy for the public to revile them.

We worried about the effect on the children, but they took it in stride. Dom made some money selling autographs of his infamous relatives.

It was a blessing in disguise that Congress had someone upon whom to vent their spleen, since it looked like it was going to be impossible to find an impartial jury to try Flynn.

Somewhere during the nine-day wonder of it all, Kel went back to work saving the world. I went back to my roach, but it didn't satisfy me. I'd acquired a taste for excitement. A taste for a spy.

I watched my bruises and wounds heal without consciously acknowledging that I was in a holding pattern, waiting and wondering what the spy would do next, now that the fat lady had not only sung, but flashed her knickers to the world.

At first I accepted that he'd be busy. The world was a big place with lots of bad guys to defeat. Then one morning, I woke up and found my bodyguards gone, an empty space with a grease spot the only sign of their recent occupation. I felt bereft. I'd become accustomed to their expressionless faces.

Even worse, it forced me to face the fact that deep down my principles and my hormones were fighting each other in a battle that didn't look like happening. Had that last, blazing kiss been a good-bye?

When the fax machine started printing, I feared the worst. I rolled my chair over and watched as boldly scrawled words gradually appeared. He had a new assignment, foreign and would be out of the country for a time, but he'd call me when he got back.

And if I believed that, I'll bet he had a bridge he could sell me . . .

I couldn't even send him a thank you note for saving my life. I'd never known his address and only had the answering service phone and a fax number.

It wasn't like I'd expected anything permanent from him. We were worlds apart, in excitement and experience, but the least he could have done is offer to have a flaming, passionate affair with me. He had no right to assume I'd turn him down and then leave without giving me the chance to tell him all the carefully thought out reasons why it would never work between us. I was so mad, if he'd shown up and I might have insisted on an affair just to prove him wrong.

But he didn't. If I hadn't had the picture of us from the paper, I might have wondered if I'd imagined the whole, incredible adventure.

When I called Marion to tell her my book was ready for her red pencil, she sensed I was a little depressed.

"I think you need to get away for a bit. Why don't you catch up with your tour?"

"My tour? The one you wanted me to go on six months ago?"

"That's right."

"You sent my tour on without me?"

Marion sighed hugely. "Of course not. It was a package deal, several children's authors were going." I could hear her flipping through some pages. "Actually, this might be good. This movie producer called. He wants to meet with you about animating Cochran. You could meet him in Vegas."

"I'm not sure I want to meet someone who wants to animate a roach. Especially not in Vegas."

She ignored that. "They're in Toledo right now. If you left in the morning you can just make the story hour at the library."

Didn't that sound like fun? I didn't want to go. I didn't want to stay. What if Kel came back? I didn't want him to think I expected him to show up. I had my pride. Or what passed for pride. What the heck. Suddenly a bunch of kids looked easier to face than my own thoughts and the echoing silence of an apartment devoid of Kel, but not free of memories of him.

I barely caught up with my fellow authors in Toledo, Ohio, and quickly came to wish I'd missed them. I'd forgotten that the teacher from the convention and my "main man, Michael" lived in Toledo. When I left the next day for Omaha, I think I was engaged to the dysfunctional fourteen year old. With my fellow authors, people who were nearly as boring as I was, I hop-scotched across the country, signing roach butts in such diverse places as Poughkeepsie and Salt Lake City. Everywhere I went, Flynn was just ahead of me, only on a better class of talk show and minus the roach tushies. It took me a two weeks to get to Las Vegas for my meeting with the roach animator.

It seemed much longer.

I was walking down the breezeway when I heard my name being called as someone who needed to pick up a courtesy telephone. I eyed it suspiciously. Courtesy and telephone were a contradiction in terms. When they called my name again, I gave in.

"Hello?" No answer. "Hello?"

"Hello, Bel," Kel said from just above my right ear.

I jumped and dropped the telephone.

"I told you not to do that!" I think my adrenal gland was out of practice, because my heart tried to pound itself right out of my chest. I turned, glad for the wall to support suddenly wobbly knees.

He grinned. "Have a good flight?"

I collected my dignity and my cool, trying to appear casually surprised, like we weren't two people who'd exchanged a volatile kiss on CNN when last we met.

"The usual. What brings you to Las Vegas?"

"I came to see you."

"Oh." I swallowed. "How did you know I'd be here?"

"We still have our ways." His blue eyes were lit with laughter and something else. He stepped closer.

There was no place for me to retreat. I tried to become one with the wall, or mash myself through it to the other side.

It was hard to think cool with my hormones fanning up a fire. Still fighting a rear guard defensive action, I arched my brows slightly, taking care not to look at him as I trailed a finger lightly down the side of the telephone. "I thought it was all over now."

"It is. Did you get my fax?" I nodded, my eyes narrowing

as I remembered his fax. He didn't seem to notice. "I got shipped out of the country the next day. I've been bouncing around the Middle East for the last month."

"I've been bouncing around the Mid West." It seemed to symbolize our vast differences. Our vast, irreconcilable differences. He was a spy. I was a Baptist. Our twains didn't know how to meet. Well, mine didn't.

"I know. I've been keeping tabs on you." He ran a finger lightly down my arm, sending shivers back up it.

"You really do have your ways, don't you?" Wonderful ways. "Kel . . ."

He put a finger over my lips, halting my words, then lightly traced their outline. "I've missed you."

"I've missed you, too," I admitted, without enthusiasm. His smile widened. "But it doesn't really matter, you know. There's no way anything could . . . I don't . . . you, me—we're too different. You're a spy and I'm . . ."

"Amazing. You're . . . amazing, Bel." He took my hand and kissed the palm, then said in a rush, "I've never known, never met anyone like you. I was going to ask you . . . to move in, but I couldn't. I couldn't do it to you. I knew you deserved better than that, so I left. I . . . just left. I didn't complain when I got sent immediately to the Mid East."

My head was spinning from his words. My heart was spinning from his smell, the look in his eyes and the feel of him seeped like honey through my veins. My veins had missed him. All of me had missed him. It had been so long. Too long. "Kel . . ."

I think he heard the denial mixed with longing in my voice.

"You can't run away from this. From us. I know. I tried. I thought a little distance would clear my head. But all that time away, all I could think about was you and how much I missed you."

"This is crazy," I whispered. My hands crept around his warm, strong neck. Now his heart beat against mine. So strong, so steady. For me?

"Maybe it is crazy, but I don't care. All I know is, I want to come home to you. Tonight. Tomorrow night. Every night. You're . . . my other half, Bel. I need you."

It was as if his words released the dam in my heart, letting the delight, the love I'd felt but been afraid to admit, even to myself. It rushed through me like a storm. "I love you, too. I love you, Kel. I love you. I didn't want to, but I do."

I think I started to cry, because he got a little blurry, but I was laughing, too. I touched him, his face, his hair, like I'd done in my imagination, but didn't have the right to do in real life.

He erased the minuscule distance between our mouths, covering mine with a deep hunger that swept away any doubt that might have lingered. He loved me. I could feel it. I could taste it. It was wonderful, even without the fireworks and cameras and danger. I felt it all the way to my toenails. And I'd just trimmed them, too. There were no cameras to record the moment, but we weren't without an audience.

"Hey, you two look like you could use my services," a brash voice intruded upon our mutual delight.

We turned slowly toward him. Some kind of shoeshine person, lean and scrungy, with an ingratiating smile stood next to us.

"I'm wearing tennis shoes," I said, dazed.

"I've already been shined." Kel sounded dazed, too.

"Not the shoes, dudes!" He turned his kit around so we could read the other side. It said: "Marriages performed. Shoe shine extra."

I had to read it several times, before it computed.

"No," I said, then with more force, "no way!"

I looked at Kel. He was grinning hopefully.

"No," I said, but even I could tell it sounded like yes.